Flamingo Flower

Flamingo Flower

David Creed

First published in Great Britain 2009
by
Robert Hale Limited

Published in Large Print 2010 by ISIS Publishing Ltd.,
7 Centremead, Osney Mead, Oxford OX2 0ES
by arrangement with
Robert Hale Limited

British Library Cataloguing in Publication Data
Creed, David, 1931–
Flamingo flower.
1. Africa, East - - Fiction.
2. Love stories.
3. Large type books.
I. Title
823.9'14–dc22

ISBN 978–0–7531–8658–9 (hb)
ISBN 978–0–7531–8659–6 (pb)

Printed and bound in Great Britain by
T. J. International Ltd., Padstow, Cornwall

When flamingoes flower on Lake Nyasa take your boat out of the water before the sun goes down.

Local saying

“Africa, it changes people”, someone says — meaning that the risks they are prepared to take with their lives become less inhibiting.

Glossary

baba, babawe	father, term of respect
baraza	local court hearing or the courthouse itself
dakika	one minute
dawa	sorcery, or materials/spells employed. Also clinical medicines
debe	large can 2-4 gallons
duka	shop
fundi	craftsman, foreman
hasua	as you say
Hodi!	Anyone home? Can I come in?
jangwa	scrub country, few trees, dry
Jumbe	headman
kahawa	coffee
kanga	colourful cotton cloth worn by women and girls, like a big stole
kansu	white cotton robe, neck to toe, often worn at mealtimes
kipande	a card issued to workmen at the start of a job recording attendance at work. Filled in daily
Kwaheri	Goodbye
Memsaab	expatriate (British) wife
Naomba Mungu	I pray God . . .
Ndiyo, 'diyo	Yes
ngoma	tribal dance, celebration
shauri	matter, business

2008

He had a comfortable second-storey flat in Clerkenwell, purchased on a long lease many years ago, before prices had gone sky-high. Nearby was an excellent Spanish restaurant, a chemist, takeaway and very adequate supermarket. It was there, one evening in April and the biting chill of winter safely past, that a neighbour, a casual acquaintance, greeted him down one of the aisles: a much younger man but already greying, who buttonholed him, eyebrows raised, and asked him, "Hey, your name's John Benning, isn't it?" and when he nodded, bringing his part-filled trolley to a halt, said, "There's a message for a John Benning in the Personal Columns of today's *Times*, did you see it?"

"No," he said. "No, but" — after a quick pause for thought and a shake of the head — "I can't think it's anything to do with me."

"Could be," the man said.

"I suppose," he agreed doubtfully. And, with a glance, "Thank you anyway. I'd better have a look" — he set off again on his rounds. When his weekly shopping was done, he found the last copy of that morning's *Times* on the stand by the checkouts and took it with him.

The message, and fairly certainly it *was* for him, asked him to ring a given number in outer London and was signed by someone called "David Morgan". He'd known a David Morgan once, a long while ago, indeed he had: a South African who, if it really were the same man, would now surely be in his eighties, half-a-dozen years older than himself. So this could still be a different David Morgan from the one he'd known and the message *not* for him — and in any case what was David doing over here? But, if he was going to get any sleep that night, Benning thought, he'd better find out, one way or the other, and set his mind at rest. Or not? Or not, in truth. To do so might only revive cruel and bitter memories, because the David Morgan he'd known had once played a crucial role in forcing upon him a career-change which, later in life, he'd never ceased to regret. Not that he blamed David for that, he'd virtually had no alternative at the time.

So, after supper, wine and brandy, over which he lingered, giving himself further time to think whether it might be better *not* to get in touch, if this were the right man, and forget the whole thing. The past was long dead and gone except in his fading memory. But, as the time passed, he realized he was sorely tempted. Surely yes, to do it and hope thereby to rekindle other closely related memories of events which had brought him joy and sorrow beyond anything he'd ever experienced before or since. To do so might well hurt terribly, but now the chance offered, and in a serious way, actually he welcomed that. Thus, his mind finally made up to take the plunge, and having cleared the table, he sat himself down by the phone on the cluttered work-surface in his study, and dialled the number provided. It was gone nine o'clock.

A woman's voice answered, middle-aged and with the faintest trace of a Jaapie accent, which had been familiar to him, no mistaking it, way back as a young man. He said quietly, "David Morgan, ma'am, is he there? May I speak to him?"

"My father?" she said in surprise. "Yes, of course, except I think he's having a snooze. Hang on a minute, if you will. Who's calling?"

"Tell him John Benning," he said, and added, "Langoro '56."

"Langoro?" she queried; but then, in a moment, "Oh yes, I remember."

"Yes, Langoro," he said again.

"All right," she murmured, and he heard the receiver being put down . . .

It took the old man four minutes to get there. First Benning heard slow footsteps and the tapping of a stick across parquet floor; then the receiver picked up and, after clearing his throat, a calm voice said, "Hullo, John."

It was almost uncanny and for a second or two he couldn't reply because whatever else might have changed in fifty years, the voice hadn't, or very little. It immediately recalled to mind, with an extraordinary clarity, a picture of the young David Morgan — always dapper, never a hair out of place — seated behind his desk in that big airy corner-office at District Headquarters when he, John Benning, had come to take his leave of his superior officer for the last time, and pick up a few things before Joseph, the station mechanic, drove him in the old government Land Rover down to the coast.

The voice in his ear said, "How are you, John?"

"Well," he said. "And you?"

There was a pause, slow breathing, then David's voice, expressionless this time, admitted, "No, not too well, I have to say. In fact the doctors don't give me more than a couple of months to live. That's why I'm here in London, to see my married daughter, on what will probably be a final visit."

"I'm sorry," Benning said. "I'm really sorry" — and waited.

"I also thought, at the back of my mind," David Morgan went on, "that, if I could contact you by any chance, I'd also like to see *you* before I die — that is if you'd agree to see me."

"Why?" John Benning asked, a little coldly.

"To tell you —" David hesitated. "To ask you how you'd got on, what you'd done with the rest of your life. In part because I felt, I've always felt, guilty."

"*Guilty*?" Benning repeated. "What have *you* got to feel guilty about? I'm the one who ought to feel guilty, and still do."

"Because maybe I could have done more to help," David said. "And maybe I should have, I suspect —"

"I've never borne you any sort of grudge, I assure you," Benning said. "It never so much as crossed my mind. I hated just about everybody — above all, myself — and my sadness was inconsolable for weeks after what happened, but then what I fully expected *must* follow did, and I accepted it, I had to, and got on. I was young enough to do that, I suppose."

"You were very brave. I didn't understand that until afterwards —"

"No, I wasn't. I even considered taking my own life, once or twice."

"But you didn't."

"No" — and, though he thought to go on, he held his tongue, waiting again.

After a few seconds, David Morgan said quietly, "You make me feel very humble, you know, thinking back, and I'd like to express my apologies to you and sincere respect, the warmth of my real feelings towards you which I thought it better to keep to myself all those years ago. I'd like to do it in person, face to face, not over the phone. Can we meet?"

He thought it over for long moments. He was very busy; had deadlines which couldn't be ignored. To dredge up the past an irrelevance now — you could say — and apart from anything else, as he'd realized well enough prior to making his call, bound to reopen old and once almost intolerably painful wounds. Was that what he really wanted? But, by so doing, could also bring back a brief period in his life filled with the sort of youthful exhilaration and happiness he'd found unattainable again as, shortly afterwards, he'd begun to suspect it would be. So, yes, he wasn't about to avoid the consequences of his earlier decision to re-establish contact if he could and, at this later stage, refuse David's invitation. Let him relive once more in the days to come — *make* time available — to celebrate and remember, as far as David's reappearance might essentially serve, those unforseen developments and passionate hours, while baring his teeth, but bowing his head, in recollection of the ultimate horrors, the dreadful ending, and all that had immediately followed. She *wouldn't* wish him to do it, he believed; had always urged him across the great divide to put her right out of his thoughts. But he was only human, she had known that too — and traded on it, for which he forgave her — and, in compassion and remorse, would surely permit him, even give him her blessing, to re-enter by way of saying a last goodbye, the world they'd discovered together for, how many days had it been? One, two? Not long anyway —

"Yes, OK," he said. "Why not, David, if you like. When and where?" It was a promise to himself to allow his memories free rein but, in any case, to be honest, there was probably no stopping them now.

Riziki kama ajali, huitambui ijapo — One's Providences are like one's Fate, and you never know when that comes

Swahili Proverb

CHAPTER ONE

They stood at the roadside in the African sun, where they could be seen — two nuns. The older, in her forties, was a strong, statuesque woman, very plain, with a snub nose and harelip long since sewn up; the other little more than a girl with a slender figure, and features — what you could see of them — undeniably attractive in a Latin way, full-lipped and dark-eyed. She was very pale, though, and didn't look well. Both wore belted white habits to the ground and their throats and cropped hair were effectively concealed by trailing white scarves and plain wimples. The younger nun had a rather battered suitcase tied with string at her feet.

They were waiting for the bus — call it a truck, but roofed over at the back, with rows of ancient seats — which would take them up the line, 120 miles, and deposit them within walking distance of their mission. They had their fares and hopefully the driver would permit them to ride with him in his cab, but if he wouldn't, or couldn't, their journey was likely to be very uncomfortable, shaken about in the open back among the cartons and bales of his load, other travellers with their bedding rolls, squalling infants and captive chickens. They weren't looking forward to it: it was just several hours of real discomfort patiently to be endured. Apart from that there was no telling whether the bus would actually come past that day or not; it had no settled timetable. So far they had waited a couple of hours for it; would wait two more and, if it still hadn't put in an appearance, return to their sister-mission in the nearby town at which they had spent the night and try again the following day. This was Southern Province, Tanganyika, in the year 1956. For many that was the way things were, and the only means available to travel far. Who knew but the bus could well have broken down somewhere since starting out from the coast that morning; it happened. If so, sooner or later it would be repaired, or another sent. They'd just have to see; word would get through to them eventually.

A few Africans passed them at the roadside, walking, and greeted them — calling them "Mama" — and were greeted in return. Then, a long-wheel-base Land Rover approached from the direction of the town and passed them at speed, trailing its cloud of dust: the first vehicle to come by since they'd begun standing there earlier. They followed it with their eyes, quickly raising ends of their scarves to cover their mouths and noses. Suddenly it braked to a halt then backed, as its dust-cloud settled, until it drew up again level with them. There was a young man in the driver's seat, leaning across and smiling at them, and the senior of the two nuns, the Mother-Sister as she was called, recognized him: the young District Officer from Langoro, the small town and District Headquarters some thirty miles beyond the turn-off to the mission to which they themselves were returning.

He switched off, threw open the car door his side, and got down, came round the bonnet and greeted them — smiling still — and extended his hand, removing his dark glasses at the same time. Tall, fair, with a rangy athletic build, he was facially deeply tanned, and seriously in need of a shave, in a sweat-stained khaki shirt unbuttoned nearly to the navel, revealing a hairy chest, plus baggy shorts, rolled-down socks and ankle-boots. He was undoubtedly good-looking in a smoothly rugged, public-school sort of way: looked tough, self-confident and boyishly alive. The older nun certainly appreciated the clean-cut male he was as, somewhat startled perhaps, the young one, who hadn't met him before, was inclined to do as well, albeit in some embarrassment. He and the senior nun shook hands — she responding without difficulty to his hard mannish grip — and he said, "Mother Livia, you're waiting for the bus? On your way back to Mtina? Would you like a lift?" And he swung round, indicating his vehicle with a gesture and an apologetic look on his face, adding, "I've got a pig in the back. It's a bit pongy sometimes, but there's room enough in the front for all three of us, I think."

"A *pig*?" Mother Livia queried, eyebrows raised.

"A pig, yes, in a crate" — he grinned — "for the agricultural people at Namwea. They asked me to bring it up for them. I've been down on the coast, a couple of days' local leave at Ras Bora."

"We don't mind a bit of pong, do we?" the older woman said, her voice cultured, southern England, authoritative, turning to the younger nun beside her, whom she now introduced. "This is Sister Carmela."

He held out his hand again, to her. "John Benning," he said. "DO Langoro. Nice to meet you, Sister." But he couldn't meet her eyes because by this time she had them lowered . . . She hesitated fractionally, before giving him her hand in return, a narrow, limp, diffident paw which moved him to hold it gently and shake it with care, until suddenly, as if she'd taken herself to task, it gripped his more strongly and she raised her eyes briefly to his with a nod and a faint smile, before looking aside. She didn't speak, and had sensational eyes, he thought — distractingly — like those of a springbok doe, pursued. The idea made him release her hand quickly and turn away, disconcerted a little that his unlooked-for arrival mightn't be as easy for her to cope with as he could have wished. He opened the passenger door of his car, pulled out a briefcase, digger hat and several loose files, tucking them under his arm, then held the door wide for the two nuns to see inside.

"Look," he said, "we can manage, I think, your case and mine in the back with the pig?"

"'Course we can," Mother Livia said. "If *you* don't mind, it's very good of you" — thinking that, with any luck the other end, John Benning would take them those extra five miles, all the way back to the mission. It wouldn't be much out of his way, they wouldn't have to walk it, and it was too good an opportunity to miss. Truly the Saviour was looking after them today, causing

Benning to come by and offer to pick them up: to Him and the Blessed Virgin her heartfelt gratitude indeed, always. "Come, Sister Carmela," she said. "Let Mr Benning have our case, then you get in first and slide across."

By the time they were in and settled — more or less comfortably, though the gear levers and handbrake meant the young one's legs were fairly cramped and one knee pressed against Mother Livia's thigh — he'd opened up the back flap of the Land Rover, dropped the tailgate and shoved their case in as far forward as he could, next to the crated pig's snout end. The poor tethered beast, a sow, stank to high heaven, but that wouldn't bother them too much as soon as they got going again. It grumbled and groaned a bit at his intrusion, and he thought, when we get to a ford I'll stop, take the cases out again and pour some water over its head and flanks through the slats in the crate — it wouldn't matter if the back of the car got a little wet — and try to relieve the thirst and discomfort it has to be suffering as best I can. The animal had to be got through alive and, if possible, in fair condition, not dead from heatstroke, dehydration, or whatever.

Having refastened the flap at the back, he stretched, yawned, did up a couple of buttons on his shirt, and returned to the front of his vehicle. He saw both nuns were seated and ready to go — so he immediately started up and set off. There was room enough, just, on the front seat for him to lean forward, back or sideways, and drive, but not without him being continually conscious of the young woman in her white habit beside him, who forbore to look at him, but whose hip and shoulder he couldn't help making contact with inadvertently sometimes as he swung the wheel, or ruts in the road bounced them together, and whose thigh and knee he brushed against with the back of his hand — and she flinching away — as, his eyes on the road, he reached across and down for the gear lever. For both of them, when it first happened, it was deeply embarrassing but, as time passed, they got used to it, accepted it couldn't be avoided, and managed to relax.

Even with the dust-laden wind of travel and all the windows open, she could smell him from time to time, the rank bitter-sweet tang of male sweat. He'd been driving since early morning in a hot car, so it wasn't surprising. At first, the scent of him nauseated her, but she fought it, didn't show it, although, to add to her discomfiture, *she* had begun to itch again, not only itch but smell, herself. She was only too aware of it and, eyes closed, prayed with all her heart that he might remain oblivious to her condition. Some infection she'd picked up in her vaginal area for reasons unknown but, in all probability and very shamingly, because she'd been guilty of caressing and playing with herself on occasion, hadn't she? God forgive her, *please God, forgive* her weakness, lascivious thoughts and memories, those lapses in self-control which had given her a nasty rash they hadn't been able to doctor at the mission. So Mother Livia, who knew perfectly well, she suspected, what might have caused her affliction, but hadn't taxed her about it as yet, had taken her down to the coast over the weekend, to the mission hospital and dispensary. There they'd given her an injection — in her bum! — and some ointment which ought, they said, to solve her problem but which, obviously, hadn't done so far. Apparently not, because here she was itching again, uncomfortable, dripping with sweat — also dreadfully tired from lack of sleep — and beside her a good-looking bloke her own age, rubbing shoulders with her sometimes, his hard male hip against hers now and then, his hand — oh *God!* — it was a long time since she had been so physically close to *any* man like this.

"You're a teaching nun, Sister?" he asked, in a while, to break the silence and to confirm his assumption, because that was what they did at Mtina; ran a pre-scondary school in a predominantly Muslim area for girls of eleven years old and up.

She started and opened her eyes, but did not turn her head to look at him. "Yes," she said evenly, and shifted a little in her seat. "Maths and other things."

"We're very lucky to have her," Mother Livia said, leaning forward; she had obviously overheard the small exchange. "She's far too highly qualified, really, but we don't, as it were, broadcast that. She's been with us nearly a year now —"

"I'm happy where I am," Carmela said softly. "The bush, the bush villages, the opportunity —"

"Like me, then," he said, glancing at her averted face, noticing her slim brown hands clasped in her lap and wondering what her history might be, what had brought her to this, so very far from home. Maybe a strong and compelling faith, plus a desire to serve, that and only that, but he found it difficult to believe. Much else, for a near-certainty, as well. Because she was, though pale and weary, seriously attractive and — indefinably — by no means unresponsive to him as a man; he felt it and it made him shy of her. He avoided her eyes, therefore, when suddenly they were turned on him, but was aware of their directness, even a hint of challenge, and concentrated on the road ahead.

"I didn't come out to Africa for the cities, the politics, the social life and so on," he said. "The outback, like Langoro — and you can't get much more outback than that, as you know — that's for me. You're needed; you can make a real difference, if you care about it enough, I suppose —"

"You're married, Mr Benning?" Mother Livia asked, leaning forward again. "I'm sorry, I forget."

"No, not yet," he said, with a shake of his head. "Actually, I'm engaged and expect to get married on my first home leave, in six months' time." He paused, before going on ruefully, "Only hope Elizabeth realizes what she's letting herself in for. It's very hard to describe in letters, the sort of existence she'll find herself part of in a place like Langoro. She's never been outside Britain before, except a couple of times to France, and here" — he shrugged — "it's not quite the same, is it?"

"No, it's not," Mother Livia agreed. They were talking across the young teaching nun, who was leaning back as far as she could and the seat permitted, so they might do so without too much difficulty above the noise of the engine. She was also listening, her eyes and head turning fractionally as one or the other spoke. "Depends so much on whether you love her unconditionally," Mother Livia continued, after a moment, "and whether she loves you in the same way. Do you? And does she?"

"Oh, I think so, yes," the young man said. "Yes indeed, I'm sure of it, on both sides. We had a year of seeing each other almost every day at college — and during vacations — before I came out here. We . . ." He hesitated, perhaps changed his mind about what he'd been going to say in present company, and finished, looking away, "We became very close."

In other words, they slept together, perhaps lived together for a while, the young nun thought, lowering her eyes again and gritting her teeth. She remained rigid in her place, breathing through her mouth, and stopped listening as, inevitably, the memories came crowding back: no power of will, no true — she believed — faith in the Redeemer, no pleas for mercy and forgiveness sufficiently strong to keep them at bay. So let her give in to them — *one last time!* — and pray that would be enough, to afford her future peace. Some hope, but never mind; this was at least a small sop to her conscience and might help. She thought of two men among others: a young husband she had worshipped and served, body and soul, to their mutual delight, but whom she had killed, *killed*, being at the wheel of the little Citroën they'd had and she half-cut at the time. The impact, the bedlam, his screaming, his tortured body, his dripping blood — and she shaken, semi-conscious but virtually unscathed — accusing her, vilifying her in vivid flashback: how could you forget that? And afterwards, eighteen months on, another guy at college, who had been a rat, and used her because she'd been lonely and afraid, until her need for him sickened her and she upped sticks and left. This man beside her, John Benning, touching her sometimes, almost intimately, reminded her of her adored husband; yes, he did, in looks and aura; she'd been aware of that from the first, at the roadside, but refused to admit it to herself. Until this moment. He reminded her also, in a different way, but particularly looks, of the rat she'd taken up with, initially in the hope of forgetting and starting a new life, only to end up miserable and disorientated again. She went for tall, fair-haired men, she supposed, with a good build and hairy chests — who didn't? — but maybe even more so in her case, with her dark genes. She was beginning to itch really unpleasantly now, and begged for it to stop. Also she needed a pee, pretty soon, and would have to ask if he went on driving on and on. Suddenly she wanted to weep; it was all getting too much, one thing after another, but clamped her jaw tight and held it back.

A couple of miles further along the road they came to a ford, lazily flowing shallow water, thirty yards wide, which, in the rains — not due for two months or more yet — would soon become impassable. He drove down to it and drew his Land Rover to a halt not far from the water's edge in the shade of an ages old mango tree. His hands on the wheel he said, "I haven't eaten since breakfast and I'm getting hungry. What about yourselves? I've got a bite of *chakula* in the back."

"We ate, thank you; we're all right," Mother Livia said, perhaps a trifle too quickly because he wasn't quite sure he believed her. She was probably thinking he'd only have brought enough for himself.

"But first," he said, pointing out the window his side to a clump of thorny acacia fifty yards off across the *jangwa*, "I'm going over there."

"Then *we'll* go over *there*," Mother Livia said, looking out through her window and selecting a small *kopje*, or outcrop of bedrock, not far off to their left, behind which they might expect to find privacy.

"Right," he said, "see you in a mo'," and swung his door open and got down. He turned away immediately — the back of his shirt dark with sweat — but stood a second or two, straightening his shoulders and working the stiffness from them — before he went off, looking about him from side to side. He relieved himself among the trees, then hung around for a minute or so, to give them a bit of time, before heading back to the car. By the time he arrived, they had already returned, and stood shoulder to shoulder the other side of the bonnet, waiting for him.

He halted, shocked, nonplussed, because it was immediately apparent that the young nun had been crying. She held a length of her scarf across the lower part of her face, above which her eyes, her expressive and beautiful eyes, were red and the eyelids swollen, while the older woman beside her looked cross, really very grim and displeased. He didn't know what to make of it, or say, so blinked, nodded, and went to the back of the vehicle, opened up, and got out the suitcases, his and theirs, which he stood on the ground beside the back wheel. Then he reached in again, past the silent crated pig — he'd do what he could for it shortly — and pulled out the cardboard carton which contained his very basic food supplies and canteens of water. He had a tin of corned beef and one of peach slices, a packet of oatmeal biscuits, all bought at a *duka* on the outskirts of Lindi first thing that morning, one dessert spoon, one tin-opener, nothing else. He lifted out a canteen of water, then in the other hand took up the two tins and, going round the front again, put them into the car where he'd been sitting on the front seat in the shade, then went back for the spoon, opener and biscuits.

The two nuns hadn't moved from by the bonnet and he looked across and said, "I won't be many minutes, you don't mind?" And, with a gesture, "Please, there's good water in the canteen here, and another one in the back. So please come and help yourselves. There's nothing to drink out of, that's all."

"We will, thank you," Mother Livia said. "But first, while you're eating, we thought we'd leave you to it and look around, stretch our legs." And to Sister Carmela and, no question but it was an order, "Fetch our case please, Sister, there's something I want from it."

"Yes, Mother," the young one said, eyes down, and turned immediately to do her bidding.

It crossed his mind to assist, get their case for them — it wasn't exactly light — but he didn't move.

Thinking no, leave it be: there was something going on here between the two of them which they'd prefer him not to know about, so OK, don't intrude, get on with having something to eat and forget the courtesies for once.

As he concentrated — hands and elbows working — on opening his tin of bully-beef, he heard the two nuns whispering together the other side of the vehicle, but couldn't see either of them or hear what was said. Then, after a minute or two, as he began digging into the opened can with his spoon and conveying the soggy but tasty contents to his mouth, he saw them again, by this time some distance back along the road, the young one who seemed to be walking fast carrying the case out in front, Mother Livia behind her. Eating, munching on a couple of dry biscuits and drinking from the canteen, he continued to keep an eye on them as they marched on and then turned into the bush, to disappear together in amongst another stand of low acacia. He trusted they wouldn't go far — surely not? Not that there were likely to be wild beasts on the prowl this time of day, but there were always snakes, scorpions and so forth, and he hoped they knew enough to be careful — of course, they did.

It was while he was spooning out the odd peach-slice from his second tin and raising the can to drink nectar from it that, with a touch of relief, he saw them returning. This time they walked side by side, the young one still carrying the case and, after leaving it at the back, they came straight to him. "Now we'd love a drink of water, may we?" Mother Livia said, smiling, obviously in a better mood than before. Immediately he held out the canteen to her, saying, “Here, please, it’s all yours, but” — he hesitated — “you have a hanky? Give the neck a wipe off, I’ve had some already.”

Taking the canteen from him, Mother Livia said equably, “No hanky; never mind, we’ll risk it,” and wiped the neck of the canteen cursorily on her sleeve before, head back, she raised the big canvas-covered container to her lips in both hands and drank plenty, before lowering the canteen and passing it to her companion while dabbing her mouth and chin with the end of her scarf. It was while the young nun was drinking that he noticed she had changed her habit for a fresh one, all starched and pristine white, showing no traces of creasing and dust and, after a moment, the penny dropped.

He looked away, turned and, reaching in under the dash below the steering wheel, extracted a packet of cigarettes, “Chapa ya Nyota”, and matches. He straightened again to light up, inhaling deeply, and then, the smoke in his left hand, faced them once more, glancing at the young one, before saying to Mother Livia with a gesture, “Please, there’s a bit of corned beef left and a few peaches. I’ve had enough, really I have, so — if you don’t mind my spoon — why don’t you and the sister polish it off? It’ll only go to waste otherwise and I’ll have to throw it away.”

Mother Livia eyed him for a second or two, in all seriousness. Then nodded slowly, and said, “You’re sure? All right then, why not, and thank you.”

So he handed her the spoon, gesturing again, offering what remained in the two tins standing on the seat, the opened packet of biscuits and stoppered canteen beside them, before taking himself off to enjoy his smoke, leaning back against the gnarled trunk of the ancient tree in the shade of which they'd pulled up.

The young nun was "periodical", of course, poor girl — he supposed. Nuns weren't exempt, they had the curse monthly like other women. Maybe the pad, or whatever else she'd been wearing, had come loose until, with the jolting about in the cab, she'd soiled her habit, her undergarment as well, her buttocks, thighs. Very unpleasant and uncomfortable, for sure — poor girl, truly. That would also account for the intermittent but persistent smell he'd picked up from her in the interior of the car as they'd travelled the miles away — foxy, animal — but done his best to ignore at the time, thinking it might be the pig, but then quite definitely *not*, it had to be her. In excuse, they were all pretty grubby, sweaty, they had to be by this hour of the day, in this heat, and he didn't suppose he actually smelt of roses himself; knew for a fact he didn't and there was no sense in denying it. He felt for her in her predicament, the extra burden she was carrying, and that they had many more miles yet to travel that day, and her condition only liable to cause her further embarrassment and discomfort. It made him think he must remember not to drive too fast and as considerately as he could, to minimize the effects of the deficiencies and hazards of the often poorly graded and maintained roadway; do everything possible to make e things a little easier for her.

By the time he had trodden out his cigarette and rejoined them, they had eaten everything he'd left, except two biscuits as a concession to "Mr Manners", and his first canteen of water was empty. He smiled and nodded., collecting things up and, without looking at the girl, said over his shoulder, "The pig, Mother, I'd like to try and sloosh it down a bit with water from the stream before we go on. Will you help me?"

"'Course we will," Mother Livia said, "Poor creature. Just tell us what to do."

Of course, he took them all the way back to Mtina, but didn't quite make it to the mission compound itself. He had had a fairly heavy weekend at the bar down at Ras Bora and out of sheer weariness and carelessness, plus the strain of many hours of hot, demanding driving that day, as night was falling and his lights probing what was little better than a track ahead, he went in the ditch. Nothing serious, they weren't travelling fast, but suddenly the Land Rover keeled over; there was a loud bang in the region of the left front wheel, the young nun let out a stifled shriek, and they stopped dead, the vehicle canted half-over on its side. He cursed, not quite under his breath, had the presence of mind to switch off, then got his door open, threw it back and scrambled out onto the road. He turned and reached in, over and down, with arm and hand, supporting himself on the doorframe, asking anxiously, "You all right, you two? You OK?" And urging, "Here, quick, hold on to of my hand and get out. Can you manage it?"

They could, one after the other, in a flurry and swish of white habits. They clambered out — he helping them — and stood at the roadside brushing themselves down and breathing hard.

"God, I'm so sorry," he said fervently. "How stupid can one get! You're sure you're both all right? Must have fallen asleep."

"A bruise or two maybe, nothing worse," Mother Livia said shortly. "You, Sister?"

"No, I'm all right," the girl said quietly. "I grabbed on to something."

Immediately Mother Livia took over. Already they could see lights — hurricane lanterns, a few hand-held torches — coming towards them from the direction of the mission; also cross-country from their right, villagers perhaps, who had heard the bang and come to see and help if required. On arrival, she marshalled them — her Swahili local and total, with a bit of humour and banter thrown in, which made them laugh — and, within ten minutes, with much heaving and grunting, cries of exhortation and further laughter, men and boys had the Land Rover back on the road and John Benning had reached in and wrenched on the handbrake. He looked all around, arms raised to shoulder height in salute and gratitude, then borrowed a man's torch and inspected his car, looking to see the extent of the damage. There was plenty. Bad denting, scraping along the left side, the passenger's window broken and the back canopy torn and in part ripped off; but worse, much worse was that the front left mudguard had been stoved in, the bumper badly buckled, and lights and everything else in that area smashed. It gave him some meagre cause for hope, though, that when he went down on one knee and shone the torch in close, up and under the twisted metal, the wheel itself seemed to be all right, the tyre also, and it looked as though he might have got away without breaking the axle.

He rose to his feet, made his way through the assembled watching people and got into the driving seat, depressed the clutch and switched on. Fine, she started. But when very cautiously he let in the clutch and attempted to move her forward, she wouldn't; there was a brutal screech of fractured metal up front and the steering wheel refused to budge either way beneath his hands, which had to mean the damage was just as serious as he'd first suspected. So he gave up immediately and switched off once more. Sat there a second or two longer, eyes closed and teeth clenched, while he upbraided himself again for his own carelessness and loss of concentration. Thought, too, that unless the government mechanic at Langoro could somehow fix what was wrong, this was surely going to cost him a packet which, with his wedding looming in the not-so-distant future, he could ill afford. Goddammit, the nearest garage with properly trained personnel and a stock of spares, which would obviously be required, was nigh on 200 miles away!

At the open window beside him, Mother Livia appeared, carrying a lantern, and he looked round.

"I'm so sorry, John," she said. "This wouldn't have happened if you hadn't given us a lift. Come along to the mission now and we'll give you a meal and a bed for the night. God willing, things may look better in the morning, in the light of day." And she added, "We're all dead beat, and you need some rest. You can have the hut in which our visiting Father sleeps when he stays with us."

"Thank you, Mother," he said wearily. "That's very kind."

CHAPTER TWO

Within the hour a young man, who would be suitably rewarded, had volunteered to carry a note from him on his bicycle, to the District Commissioner at Langoro. He was equipped for it with front and rear lights, so he said, and could spend the night in the town with a friend. So his note should be in the DC's hands by ten or half-past that evening if all went well. It reported his accident briefly and that he was staying the night at Mtina, and asked David Morgan please to despatch Joseph Ulaya, the station mechanic, in the government Land Rover, to him first thing in the morning.

From the moment of his going off the road, Mother Livia, though surely very tired herself, had proved a tower of strength and authority. She organized men with long poles from which the crated pig — grumbling occasionally but obviously a survivor — was slung on ropes and then transported on men's shoulders to the mission compound. She co-opted a trusted villager to sleep in the vehicle and guard it during the hours of darkness, and another to bring the man food and water. She called on a couple of boys to carry their bags and accompany them and light their way as they set off along the half-mile of track which remained to the mission buildings. And in the half-hour, a little longer, which all this took to accomplish, John Benning saw no sign of the younger nun, Carmela, and presumed therefore she'd been sent on ahead.

On arrival, they went in through the main entrance, an archway between lockable gates of heavy planking — now thrown wide — in the high wattle-and-daub and glass-tapped walls surrounding the mission enclave. Lights, of candles and lanterns, showed here and there in the open windows of various thatched-roofed buildings ahead, and Mother Livia led him straight to the one which turned out to be the refectory, where she invited him to sit down on one of the six or so upright chairs either side and at the head of a long solidly made dark wood table. Through a doorway to his right, a young African girl, in a long skirt, *kanga* and headscarf, appeared immediately carrying a tin tray on which were big glasses of sweetened limejuice and cool water which, with a smile and a quiet greeting, she set down on the table between himself and Mother Livia who had taken a seat opposite. Very welcome. Mother Livia thanked the young girl, whom she called La'ali, who then withdrew. Through the same doorway by which she'd departed drifted a wonderfully appetizing aroma of meaty cooking, and all at once, from outside and not far away, a church bell tolled a couple of times, a deep resounding note, summoning worshippers to prayer. He drank his limejuice gratefully while, by lamplight, getting out a pen and a pad of paper from his briefcase he composed his note to the DC; put it in an envelope finally and passed it across into Mother Livia's hand.

She got to her feet, saying, "This'll get off straightaway," and, as he rose with her, said "I'll show you to your room now, John, and have someone bring you a *debe* of water to wash. Take your time, supper will be half an hour yet at least."

"I'm sorry to put you to so much trouble," he said, as he accompanied her to the door.

"Nice to have you with us," she said, without affectation. "And you did us a real favour, picking us up at the roadside this morning."

She had brought the lamp with her and led the way across the compound past two big, open-sided, thatched-roofed classrooms, a long hut which might well be the girls' latrines, to a rondavel standing by itself within yards of the western wall. The door, of framed coconut matting, was shut but unlocked and she pushed it open and preceded him inside. In the last hour it had been got ready against his arrival (by Sister Carmela?): a hurricane lantern, burning low, stood on a centrally placed deal table, an upright chair beside it; there was an old chest of drawers not far away against the wall, a carved and hand-painted crucifix above it, and the murram floor looked very recently swept. To his left the bed, of axed timber and plaited rope, with a canvas-covered and flock-filled mattress, had been made up with clean white sheets and a pillow-case, and the mosquito-net, suspended from a roofbeam, lowered and tucked in all round. At the foot of the bed they had deposited his suitcase. Mother Livia passed by it to an open doorway at the back, inviting him to follow. Raising her lamp to shoulder height she showed him the interior of the little annexe beyond, the marble-topped washstand with mirror, china basin and hanging towel, the thunderbox to the right; to the left an oblong of concrete floor with raised edges and a drainage hole in one corner — on which you could stand and either pour water over your head with a baler or sponge yourself down.

"All right?" she asked, turning to him.

"Fine, Mother," he said. "I'm very grateful."

"Hot water will be here directly," she said, moving back across the circular room. "One of our girls will leave it outside the door. When you're ready, come on over to the refectory. If I'm not there, just introduce yourself to the others, they know you're here."

"I will," he said, and, "I won't be many minutes." Following her as far as the table, he picked up his lamp and adjusted the wick, so that at once the room was filled with yellow light and his shadow thrown in stark contrast over the wall behind him.

On her way out Mother Livia paused a moment in the doorway and glanced back at him: eyes narrowed he was still fiddling with the wick and making sure the lamp didn't smoke. Truly, she thought, he was a good-looking boy — tired, unshaven and dishevelled though he might be just now, or perhaps partly because of that. His face was youthful but self-assured without being cocky, outgoing and ready for anything; his build that of an athlete, loose-limbed and broad in the shoulder, and his manners — as had been revealed that day — were near-perfect, which only added to his appeal. Already he was making a name for himself in this district, she knew; Africans both liked and were coming to trust him and for that she saw every reason to like and respect him as well. No wonder Sister Carmela had been smitten, she thought, as she closed the door of the rondavel behind her and headed away in the direction of her own quarters. His looks, his personal magnetism, his close physical proximity in the car had been too much for her at first, and she had lusted after him, her imagination running riot, as she had blurted out and confessed, tearfully, when they had stopped by the roadside at that ford. And she, Mother Livia, hadn't been as gentle and understanding with the girl then as she might have been, had she? No, she'd been cutting and dismissive. But, on the other hand, in the end, that was almost certainly for the best, and in the girl's long-term interests. She had chosen to become a nun, a handmaid of Christ; had so far given every impression of being both committed to and fulfilled by all that was required of her at Mtina. And though very probably she was prone to occasional impure thoughts and memories, leading to lapses in self-control, if her infection were anything to go by, she *must* and *would*, through prayer and penitence, and their Saviour's loving intervention, also with the help and guidance of herself and their visiting pastor, learn to master her indiscipline and weakness, root it out of her system, and permit no thoughts of that kind to plague her further. Mother Livia knew from experience it could take time and, on her own part, patience — *not* her strong suit, as a rule, and she knew that also, equally well. It was a failing which had dogged her through life thus far, sometimes to her advantage, often not. That the young man in question would be gone, one way or another, in the morning and the girl unlikely to set eyes on him again, could only make it easier for Carmela to live up to the tenets of her vocation, hold fast to the vows they'd all of them made, in Carmela's case comparatively recently, in her own, twenty-odd years before.

He woke in the night, took a few seconds to remember where he was and what had brought him there: a moment's unpardonable negligence, and his car — his nearly-new car, bought second-hand, but with not too many miles on the clock: it had quickly become an integral and enjoyable accessory to his life at Langoro — his ever-reliable, well-nigh indispensible car badly damaged and immobilized, Goddammit. With the result that, with little doubt, it would require extensive, time-consuming and costly repair. He wouldn't lack for transport: there was always the station Land Rover — battered if meticulously maintained rattletrap though it was — but sometimes the Doctor needed it, then again the Road Foreman, the one Goan, the other Seychellois, and his freedom to come and go more or less as he pleased and his job dictated, was bound to be curtailed. So much now depended on Joseph Ulaya, the station mechanic, in the morning. A mission-educated Christian from the north, and entirely self-trained, he had an almost uncanny affinity with all machinery, whether powered by gasoline, battery or clockwork — he'd been known to fix faulty wristwatches, portable radios and typewriters among other things, with or without the benefit of manuals or spares — and it was just possible that *he* might have the skills required to improvise, reconnect, weld, panel-beat or otherwise restore his vehicle, to the extent of getting it back on the road. In this case, from the nature and evident severity of the damage sustained, Benning couldn't really see that happening, but with Joseph on hand to cast his eye over what needed to be done, then perhaps trying his hand at doing it, you never knew. And he could only fervently pray . . .

He had gone along to the refectory, he recalled — after a shave and a wash-down and getting into a clean shirt and khaki shorts — there to be welcomed by a couple of bubbly Irish nuns. Round-faced and toothy both, excited, talkative and gauche, they could almost have been twins and vied with one another to bring him a cool drink, have news of where he'd been and why, commiserate with him on his accident and the damage to his vehicle, then express their complete confidence that in the morning and with God's help, Joseph Ulaya — who was personally known to them and had come out to resuscitate the mission gramophone not so long ago — would have it repaired and as good as new in no time. He only hoped that, conceivably, they'd be proved right, and responded to their enthusiasm and faith in the benevolence of the Almighty, not to mention the expertise of Joseph Ulaya — which had given his spirits a much-needed lift. Only when the arrival of Mother Livia had imposed a certain order into the proceedings had the two of them quietened down a little in deference.

They took their places at table, Mother Livia at the head, he on her right, the two Irish nuns facing him, and a grace was said in Latin. Then, served by La'ali, the attractive young African girl, their meal was brought in, a considerable and tasty repast into which they all tucked in. They were all hungry and this was their principal meal of the day. A thick vegetable soup to start with, then a goat's-meat goulash with country rice, pumpkin and green beans, followed by slices of papaya, cane sugar and fresh limes. To begin with little was said — this was definitely serious business — he only remarking from time to time on how delicious everything was, they encouraging him to have more and pile his plate high which, deprecatingly, he did, since there appeared to be plenty for all. With the arrival of their fruit and mugs of tea, everyone settled back a bit, and he came out with the question which had been in his thoughts since the commencement of their meal.

"Sister Carmela?" he asked. "She's not joining you tonight? She's not sick or anything, I trust."

"She's not too well, no," Mother Livia said. "A headache, travel-weariness, that's all, I think. She asked me to make her excuses to you, if you wondered about her absence."

"I'm sorry," he said. "In a year or two we'll have a decent tarmac road in Southern Province, right the way through from Lindi to Mingida and, golly, one looks forward to the day. It'll make things so much easier all round."

"But I don't suppose you'll still be here to see it, will you?" she said quietly. Pleasantly enough, but — ? All at once he realized he knew very little about her — this unquestionably able and impressive woman they called the Mother-Sister — only that, by all accounts, she ran a successful school and mission in an isolated spot and difficult circumstances. Only once thus far — by the ford where the three of them had stopped for food — had he caught a glimpse, perhaps, of the hard, uncompromising, possibly cynical disciplinarian who held the enterprise of Mtina together and drove it on. He became aware that the two Irish nuns had fallen silent, and that there was definitely a certain tension in the air, which, a touch uncomfortably, he did his best to dispel.

"Oh yes, that's true, I'm afraid. I only wish it weren't. I'm almost certain to be transferred sooner or later, probably as soon as I return from my coming leave. But, you never know" — he smiled and shrugged, looking around — "I could get lucky and they'll send me back here for another tour."

"I pray your wish may be granted," Mother Livia said, with genuine kindness and, indeed, affection, and the tension he'd felt a moment ago — or had he imagined it? — was immediately gone. But it left its mark, as if his eyes had been opened a fraction wider and any evaluation of her true character put on hold, in the light of what had just, apparently, occurred . . .

In the night he heard a noise, outside his rondavel, near or far away it was hard to tell, but he lay still beneath his net, and listened. The pig perhaps, grown restless in its crate, poor beast, which had been set down in the lee of the compound wall a dozen yards from his door. After supper in the refectory, the nuns had accompanied him and held lamps and torches while he had done what he could for it. He had unfastened the padlock and lowered the slatted planking on its hinges and placed a basin of water where the tethered animal could get at it, also a tray laden with scraps and peelings from the refectory kitchen. He had stood back and watched after that while, grunting, snuffling and straining against its bonds, slobbering and scattering scraps to right and left, the pig drank and ate, its little eyes glinting in the lights, its huge ears giving it some respite from the glare. Poor bloody creature, really, but at least, he was relieved to see, it looked nowhere near collapse or on its last legs, as he'd feared. Tough pig, indeed.

The noise came again: *not* the pig, but from much further away, the other end of the compound and very faint. He attempted to analyse it, but couldn't; only realized, when it recurred once more, that it sounded like a distant cry of pain. What the hell? Surely someone else as well as himself had heard it? It had come from *within* the compound, not from beyond the walls, he was pretty sure of that. But perhaps they were all fast asleep by this time; it was just on 2a.m., his watch said. *Not* his business, of course, whatever it might be; anyway, the sound, or cry, whatever its cause, wasn't repeated: the silence of the night continued on and remained unbroken. Suddenly wide awake, lying there in the darkness of his hut, he was tempted, nevertheless, to go and investigate, quietly, without waking anyone for the moment, in case it amounted to nothing of any consequence. But if it was an intruder? For Heaven's sake, someone ought to raise the alarm, call in the watchman from outside the walls who was armed with a muzzle-loader, he'd been told — where was he? — so that, between them they might confront and drive out whatever had got in. A leopard? Could it be? Surely not: the walls were too high and topped with broken glass, the gates locked and impenetrable — unless someone had left them open. Now he came to think of it that cry he'd heard hadn't sounded like one made by any animal, either. No, fairly certainly not. Which left the possibility —

He got up, dressed quickly by torchlight, shook out, got into and laced up his boots. Then he knelt down at the foot of his bed, unlocked and delved into his suitcase. He found and lifted out a custom-made oilskin wallet; in it a sealed box — flat, oblong and metallic — which contained the broken-down components of a Luger 7mm handgun (German senior officers for the use of) a present to him from his father who, until recently, had been a serving soldier in occupied Europe and had passed it on to his son on his departure for Africa, and which, from habit, Benning always took with him when travelling far afield and liable to be away overnight. He extracted it piece by piece from its case and rapidly assembled it, before snapping a magazine of shells into the butt and thumbing back the safety-catch. A formidable weapon, comparatively light and beautifully engineered, it would stop more or less anything short of an elephant and, though he had never yet had cause to use it in earnest, he had practised with it from time to time and felt comfortable with it in his hand.

Thus equipped, he rose to his feet and made for the door and, as he did so, that wailing cry in the distance came once more. An enigmatic and rather unearthly sound, it stopped him momentarily in his tracks. But he unbarred the door, opened it and, as a precaution, shone his torch — a long fourcell affair and the batteries almost new — all around, before stepping outside into the misty night air. There was little to see: the well-trodden path at his feet, patches of thin grass to either side, the classrooms, if that was what they were, long low buildings, further away and barely distinguishable, the beam of his torch not reaching so far. Overhead, the night was freckled with stars, but apart from those there was no light visible anywhere — except *one*! At the other end of the compound in the vicinity of the church, a light shone out, then disappeared briefly; shone out again and held steady.

He went towards it, his weapon in his right hand at his side — safety-catch off — the torch in the other, lighting his way. Listening; all the time listening, and keeping watch, sweeping the beam of his torch right and left, not to be caught unawares. If there was an intruder — a dangerous animal — he knew he was putting himself at considerable risk venturing out like this, but, to hell with it. By this time his curiosity was aroused; he was the only man around here, barring the watchman, and he wasn't turning back yet. From a little way off, in passing, he shone his torch over the crated pig under the wall, but it was either comatose or asleep and made no sound. There was no sound either from anywhere within the compound ahead — distant drumming barely audible, that's all, an *ngoma* in progress at some village miles away to the north.

The light was coming from inside the church itself and, as soon as he was sure of that, he headed directly for it, passing a well covered over with palm-fronds, a low wall around it, then tended plots of sweet potato, beans and young marrows. The shadowy outlines of other ancilliary mission buildings — the refectory and kitchens, nuns' quarters, office and storerooms — were all silent and dark on his left. The grass underfoot muffled the sound of his footfalls. As he approached the light, all at once and in growing unease he slowed down, halted and switched off his torch. He didn't want to betray his presence unnecessarily, was ready to beat a silent, circumspect retreat — until he was sure whoever was inside the church was there for legitimate reasons. That there *was* someone within the building — maybe more than one — and that the nuns didn't merely leave a lamp burning there overnight, wasn't open to question in his mind; he'd seen the light vanish then shine out again, once, had he not?

After looking around carefully, listening again, and neither seeing nor hearing anything untoward, he went forward, using the light through the open window ahead to pick his way. Facing him, up a couple of steps, were the closed church doors, the angled thatch of the roof above them against the starry sky, and the light, probably from more than one lamp within, shone out through the single unshuttered window to the right. Cautiously, not making straight for them but circling a little, he mounted the steps, crossed silently to the window and, leaning forward, looked in. Immediately he pulled back, wincing and catching his breath, because what he had glimpsed going on — or having already taken place — in the interior of the church, beyond the twin lines of benches and before the rudimentary altar, looked to be so *unthinkable*, and *appalling*, that he seriously suspected his eyes must have been deceiving him, or, to put it another way, that he must have misread the scene entirely. So, after a few seconds and gathering himself together, he leaned forward again and took a second look.

Two lamps were burning in the little church, one close by him on a table near the barred-shut doors to his left, the other atop the altar itself, beneath but to one side of an almost life-sized figure of the crucified Christ — arms stretched wide, near-naked body hanging limp, head drooping and crowned with thorns and blood trickling down from its inflicted wounds, affixed to the whitewashed wall above.

Before the altar, under the glazed eyes of the crucified One, stood Mother Livia, her back to him, the sleeve of her habit rolled up above the elbow, and a *kiboko* — a five foot long, tapering rawhide whip of merciless repute — in the grip of her right hand and dangling from it to the floor. Across the steps leading up to the altar, at her feet, sprawled the stricken, prostrated, half-naked body of a girl. Carmela, a shift covering her from the waist down. She had been scourged, the bloody lines of the whipping she'd undergone cross-hatched into the tender flesh of her upper arms, slender back and shoulders. Shocked, staring still and incredulous, Benning was about to react: to shout out, remonstrate, intervene, *but did not*.

Because he'd noticed, first, the two Irish nuns, so friendly and welcoming at suppertime, watching, arms folded and faces grim, seated side by side on a bench nearby. Then, that Sister Carmela was slowly, shakily, getting to her feet. Straightening up and lifting her cropped head, her eyes importuning the facsimile of Christ Crucified above her, her shapely arms raised to it in supplication. After a moment's pause she turned her head and urged the tall, strapping woman holding the whip, "*Again*, Mother Livia. Please, *again*!" Her voice rising in entreaty and a wild, demented resolve. "You *mustn't stop, go on*! I can take it, I *can*." And, with that, she went up closer to the cloth-covered altar, took hold of it, her bare arms out wide in imitation of the hanging figure above her and bent her back in readiness.

"In the name of God the Father, Son, and Holy Spirit," Mother Livia intoned, in a cold unemotional voice. She followed the girl to the altar before, stepping to one side, she set herself, drew back her arm, raised her whip and swung, the crack of the lash, as it struck home, forcing utterance of the same cry of agony, the same shriek of suffering, as he had picked up from afar minutes ago in the darkness of his rondavel. It wasn't repeated; the scourging went on — one deliberate laying on of the lash giving way to the next. But, though her whole body flinched and trembled, the girl held still and no further sound escaped her lips. Then, close to passing out no doubt, and unable to endure any more, her grip on the altar-table slackened, her legs gave way, and she slumped keening to her knees, crouching low over them, her arms raised to cover and protect her head and neck. The two Irish nuns leapt up and rushed forward; Mother Livia threw down her whip, and the three of them, murmuring together in concern, lifted the sobbing girl to her feet, began leading her, supporting her, to one side.

Not wanting to risk being seen, Benning stepped back, away from the window, almost overbalancing as he went down the steps, but he kept his feet and didn't fall. He retreated, head down, circling again but hardly aware of what he did. Thinking, "What do I do, about *this*? This is way beyond my comprehension and experience — horrifying, frightful! What *should* I do? I cannot let this pass, *must* not, but, before doing anything else, I have to seek advice, share a little of the burden of being a witness. But will anyone believe me when I tell them? I can hardly believe it myself, even now. Such deliberate barbarity, such fearsome punishment meted out at *her* insistence, on the pliant and unresistant body of a young girl — by *nuns* on one of their own! Surely nothing in this world can justify such treatment? Why? Why was it done? How had she transgressed? I've no idea. And why *didn't* I shout out and stop it when I had the chance and the bloody ritual began again? I should have done, but I didn't; why was that? Was I mesmerized? Did I funk it? Was I so unnerved and entranced by the sight of what was taking place that I was struck dumb, unable to get a word out? God forgive me, has to be something of the sort, and it does me no credit at all. So, when I take this matter further, as I have to do, better perhaps I say nothing about that side of things — my own inadequacy in the face of undreamt-of evil. No, much better I leave that out. That girl, poor abused and distracted creature, she suffered more and for longer, because of what I did or didn't do. Even if at the time she was begging for it, for me that's not even the semblance of an excuse."

Quickly, making minimal use of his torch, he found his way back to his rondavel and, after a while, returned to bed. But could not sleep.

CHAPTER THREE

He went along to the refectory at 7.30. By that time he'd finally made up his mind that whoever he met there, he'd say nothing, give no hint that he knew about the events he'd witnessed in the early hours. He would pretend that, exhausted, he'd slept the night away, as perhaps they'd confidently expected him to do. He didn't like the thought of keeping quiet, wasn't sure, either, whether he'd find it at all easy to act normally, as if wholly unaware of what had gone on, but, it seemed to him, this was his only responsible course until he'd carried his story to the DC and discussed with him the way forward.

In the event, though, he met no one in the refectory but La'ali. The young African girl had been waiting for him and welcomed him to the table. She served him a substantial breakfast — pumelo, maize porridge, followed by fried eggs on toasted bread and salty butter — and while she did, and he ate and drank his tea, they talked. He asked where everyone was.

Gone to Mtina village, she said, her birthplace, about two girls who hadn't turned up to school all last week. They were about to be married and the nuns had gone to see their fathers to try to persuade them to allow the girls at least to finish the current stage of their education.

"Sister Carmela?" he queried. "She went with the others?"

"Oh yes," La'ali said. "She's better this morning."

Better, he thought, how could she be *better*? Or was it that, with him still around, the other nuns had deemed it advisable to drag her along with them thereby leaving nothing to chance? My God, he thought, but I'm beginning to think of these nuns — Mother Livia especially — as monsters; at the same time being aware that for reasons only to be guessed at, that description might not quite fit the case. "*Go on*!" the half-naked girl had cried in the night, her back already lacerated and bloody. "*Don't stop*! I can take it, I *can*" — and those words, that scene, he was never likely to forget. He was still inclined, he supposed, to give these nuns — any nuns — the benefit of whatever possible doubts there might be, but suspected he was being naïve. He surely was, wasn't he? Towards the end of his meal, while he was downing a final cup of tea, he said to La'ali — her name the Arabic for "Pearls" — "Mother Livia, the other nuns here, the people round about, *your* people, they accept the mission in their midst, and respect the nuns for what they do?"

"Oh *yes*!" La'ali said, without even a fraction of a second's hesitation. "They are good, good women, and teach the girls many things of practical use to them apart from giving them extra schooling. They never try to convert them to Christianity. Some, like myself, have converted, but then I'm an orphan and no one minds."

She paused thoughtfully, before going on, "When they first came, years ago, the *jumbes* and religious sheikhs didn't like it that the nuns should be here and made things quite difficult for them. But now all that is changed. It has been mostly Mother Livia's doing, I think. She is a Mother-Sister of much experience, strong character and good sense, and the people's leaders talk to her, consult her — *rely* on her — quite often, when they are unsure of what's to be done for the best." Again La'ali smiled and shook her head. Concluded, "Oh, Mother Livia, she's outstanding, you know and, for me, it's an honour to be allowed to serve her."

After that he didn't say any more or ask any more questions. He finished his breakfast and, after thanking her, he returned to his quarters to wait for Joseph Ulaya.

Joseph was sturdily built, dressed in overalls and, apart from the deep-brown colour of his skin and crinkly hair, he could have belonged to almost any ethnic group. Forty years old, he had a good face, composed, tolerant, self-reliant, and a low, attractive voice which made you trust him. He arrived in the station Land Rover at 8.30, with his tools, jack, welding equipment and so on, in the back and, having heard him coming, John Benning was there to meet him at the gate. Strangely enough, and perhaps delightfully, he thought afterwards, having other things on his mind at the time, La'ali was also on hand to greet him, doing so with obvious warmth coupled with a certain shyness, to which Joseph responded gravely but without disguising that it pleased him to see her again.

The two of them drove off at once, back the way Joseph had come, to the stranded car, where they shook hands with the greying veteran who was still at his post guarding the vehicle. Then, as slowly, by ones and twos, spectators from nearby villages gathered, and John Benning crouched beside him, Joseph rolled on to his back and eased himself under the chassis to make his preliminary survey of the damage.

It took him five long minutes and once he called out, his voice muffled, "*Nipe pis-pisi*". Benning opened and rummaged about in his toolbag, until he found a big screwdriver and passed it into Joseph's waiting hand. After that came the sounds of tinkering and once a slab of caked mud plopped to the ground beside the wheel. Eventually Joseph slid out from under again and got to his feet, slapping dust from his overalls. Benning also stood up beside him and, after a moment asked, "What d'you think?"

"It's not good, bwana," Joseph said quietly. He turned away to spit out some dust and clear his throat. "Steering rod's bent, shock-absorber mounting broken loose, brake-fluid pipe gone, much damage to lights and metal."

"Oh hell," Benning breathed. Then, "I'll have to get her down to Lindi, will I?"

"Maybe yes," Joseph said. "But just wait a bit, until I get the jack under her, and really see what we're up against." He shrugged. "Perhaps, who knows . . ."

"I beg you," John Benning said, "do everything you can. Even if she can be *towed* carefully down to the coast, that would be something, a great deal, in fact."

"Leave it to me, bwana," Joseph said, and gave one of his rare smiles, as if the challenge facing him really sparked his interest. "If anything can be done, I'll do it, I promise you. But it's likely to take time."

"You need my help?" John Benning asked. "If not, I should get back to Langoro."

"No, you go then," Joseph said and, indicating the group of people watching, "They help me, if I need it."

"I'll be back for you later this afternoon," John said. "Or if I can't come, I'll send someone out. Will that be all right?"

"Fine, bwana," Joseph said. "At midday I'll take my food at the mission, they know me there."

"All right then, and thank you," Benning said, turning away.

With the help of bystanders, they unloaded the old station Land Rover of Joseph's equipment. Then, after clasping his hand and wishing him luck, John Benning drove away, back to the mission.

There, the nuns had returned from their visit to Mtina — an unsuccessful one, La'ali told him sadly — and, laughing and talking in small groups, a score of girls, aged ten years old to sixteen, hung about in the vicinity of the classrooms, books and satchels under their arms, in readiness for the start of classes at ten. Going immediately to his rondavel Benning packed up his things, left his case beside the unmade bed, then went in search of Mother Livia. He had no desire at all to see her, but it had to be done.

He found her in her office — a whitewashed single-room shack with a thatched roof not far from the church — and with her, he could see through the open doorway as he approached, facing her superior and seated on an upright chair, the white-clad figure of Sister Carmela. This stopped him momentarily in mid-stride. He hesitated and almost turned back, but then, getting his surprise, confusion, pity (but also curiosity) under some sort of control, went forward slowly to the doorway, where he paused, looking in at the girl, her back to him, her cropped head bare, before murmuring "*Hodi*!" and asking Mother Livia's permission to enter.

"Of course, John, come," she said, and raised smiling eyes to his across the bright barely furnished little room, pushing aside some papers she'd been reading. "How're things with your car? Joseph arrived, so they tell me."

He crossed the floor and stood at Sister Carmela's shoulder, and met — it wasn't easy but he managed it — Mother Livia's motherly and approving appraisal of him as he halted before her. "It's a bit early to say," he said quietly. "It doesn't look too good, I'm afraid, but I can only hope Joseph will be able to work one of his miracles." He added, "I better get off to Langoro now, to try to save that pig, apart from anything else, but I'll return this evening, if I may, to see how he's got on, and then take him back with me before nightfall."

"We'll look after him until then," Mother Livia said. "But, as of now" — she rose to her feet — "I expect you'd like us to help you get the pig loaded, wouldn't you?"

"Please. That would be very kind," he said. But, prior to turning away, he glanced down at Sister Carmela; it was impossible to go on ignoring her. She was staring up at him, her dark eyes ravaged and quite plainly revealing her continuing pain and suffering. His heart went out to her in sympathy — that, before anything else. "You're feeling better, Sister," he asked, after a moment. "Is that right?"

"Much better, thank you," she said huskily, and nodded. But then, as he continued to watch her, perhaps betraying a little of his unspoken disbelief, the expression in her eyes as they watched him in return, changed, and the look she gave him before quickly lowering her gaze, disconcerted him, dismayed and bewildered him, because, it seemed to him, it was one of virulent and unqualified dislike. Surely not, but, if so, *why*, for Heaven's sake? He couldn't fathom it, her attitude to him made no sense — did it? He swung round to escape her and follow Mother Livia who was already at the door. He looked back once, though, before he went out, to see the young nun still sitting where he'd left her, her head turned and her eyes on him once more. And this time they seemed to be attempting to convey something quite different: a plea for forgiveness and commiseration, perhaps; also that she didn't blame him — for exactly what he couldn't even begin to hazard a guess. She hadn't seen him, or been aware of his presence nearby during the night — *no one* had. Nor had anyone seen him returning to his rondavel afterwards, he was as certain of that as made no difference, or someone would have said. So, apart from those horrific events in the small hours, the girl must have something else on her mind concerning him to account for the strangeness and apparent ambivalence of her behaviour.

Outside, he took a deep breath, shook his head and did his best to shut her out of his thoughts. It was difficult, but he succeeded, because Mother Livia was waiting for him impatiently and he had things to do and get on with straightaway. He left her and strode the length of the compound to the main gate; got into his borrowed Land Rover and backed it up to the entrance. Then, with a gaggle of laughing girls under Mother Livia's direction to provide the muscle required, while he largely looked on, he accompanied the transport of the crated animal on long poles as before from where it had spent the night near his sleeping quarters, to the gate, when he supervised getting it into the back of the car. Apart from smelling even worse than the previous day, it looked to be all right — still emitted protesting grunts and squeals from time to time. Its resilience and fortitude filled him with nothing but admiration. After more ropes had been brought and they'd tied its crate securely in place, he took his leave of Mother Livia because he was eager to be gone. Managing a smile while he thanked her for her help and hospitality, he shook her briefly by the hand; then, with a wave and smiling words of thanks to the girls still gathered round, he picked up his case which one of them had brought and stuffed it into the car in the passenger footwell. After that he drove off with a surge of relief, sounding his horn a couple of times in parting. Half a mile along the road he came upon his own vehicle, jacked up and bonnet wide open but, though he pulled up and waited a moment or two, Joseph didn't put in an appearance.

He drove, and thought, and drove some more, until he reached the main road, when he turned on to it in the direction of Langoro. But immediately he drew in to the side of the road and stopped, lighting up a cigrette and taking himself to task, because he was fully aware that since leaving the mission, he'd been driving very badly and the last thing he needed was another accident.

That girl back there, *she*, that nun — that maltreated, driven and, to him, wholly enigmatic young woman — when he'd seen her last, in Mother Livia's office, she'd been trying to tell him something, explain herself; that much he surmised if nothing else. Somewhere in this dreadful breakdown in religious tolerance and observance at the mission was a crucial point, and he was missing it, not only in his perception of it but, as a consequence, interpretation as well. All he intuited from his vivid memory of the night's events plus the girl's changes of mood barely an hour ago, was that here was a naturally gifted, grossly persecuted young woman; one who was indeed desirable, both in looks and poignant allure as much as by reason of her lissom shapely figure, who appealed to him — in both meanings of the word — and invited his compassion. He couldn't deny it. One who had been brutally whipped and abused by a stronger, dominant superior but, incomprehensibly enough, found that acceptable — because she'd sinned? — at the same time making it clear she laid the responsibility for her predicament at least partly on *his* shoulders. And if he couldn't deduce a possible reason for that, he suspected, couldn't bring himself at any rate to believe it, then he was being thick, had his head in the sand, and had better bloody well grow up!

But, as of this moment, and for the foreseeable future, there were only two things he had to do: make quite certain that, for both their sakes she didn't see hide nor hair of him again or, at least, for many days to come; secondly — a thousand times more important — that the sort of cruel punishment meted out to her, or anything like it, which he had witnessed during the night, must never be permitted to happen again. And if that meant the prosecution and disciplining of Mother Livia, the summary banishment of that formidable and heartless woman to beyond the pale of her vocation, even the closure of the mission at Mtina, so be it. With David Morgan's backing and, he was quite certain, horrified and unstinting approval, something had to be done and he, John Benning, was determined it should be. The situation back there, whatever had sparked it to life, couldn't be allowed to continue.

After a while he threw away the butt of his cigarette, started up and headed for home. But still, inevitably, he went on thinking about Carmela. My God, but they were supposed to be Christians at that mission — not idolaters — women, the gentler sex, missionaries, *nuns*!

In a way, he supposed, all that had taken place out there sowed doubts in his mind about the role, the justification for the presence of the European in Africa, and he hated to have his deepest convictions — idealistic and naive as they might be at times — undermined to this extent.

CHAPTER FOUR

The town straggled up a long sloping hillside, a big native village at its foot by the river, then an ascending line of Indian *dukas* either side of the main road, beneath ancient and spreading tamarind trees backed by bush until it reached an extensive plateau, the rim of which overlooked the town and the rolling tree-covered hills and plains beyond. There, either side of the road which continued on all the way to Mingida, 160 miles to the west, were sited the District Office and courthouse, Native Treasury, prison, carpenter's shop, police lines and hospital — red brick or stuccoed buildings all, with corrugated iron roofs — plus, beyond those, on the southern side, the bungalows assigned to the DC, DO, Agricultural Officer, Doctor and Road Foreman, the latter two smaller than the others and roofed with thatch. Of all these, John Benning's happened to be the newest and was sited in some isolation on the far side of the rarely used and rudimentary grass airstrip.

It was no more than five rooms in a line with a deep veranda running the whole length of it, looking out towards the rest of the station, with a cookhouse and servants' quarters in small separate breezeblock buildings out at the back. With the District Office still fifty yards ahead on his right, Benning turned left off the main road and followed the murram track leading in its direction; passed the DC's and AO's bungalows — again on his left, partly concealed by mature tamarind and the occasional casuarina — also the little-used tennis court, before driving across the airstrip, and sixty yards beyond, to draw up a short distance from his door. At the top of the two steps leading up to the veranda stood his cook/houseboy, a local man called Salim; beside him the kid Kaisi, the son of one of the District Office messengers, who actually did most of the work and was learning his future trade. Both wore loose white shirts over checkered cloths tied at the hip, and were smiling broadly in welcome. He got down and Salim came to meet him: he was not a young man, soft-spoken, competent and trusted. They greeted each other warmly, but by this time the look on Salim's face had changed to one of sincere condolence, his eyes on the vehicle in which Benning had arrived.

"*Gari yako*?" he asked. Your car? And he added, "We heard about it in the night. *Nasikitika sana*, bwana" — I'm very sorry. He shook his head. "Is it bad?"

"Yes, I think so," Benning said, and made a face. "But Joseph's out there now, and I'll know for certain this evening."

"*Naomba Mungu* —" Salim began, but Benning cut him short without giving offence, saying wearily, "Never mind, *baba*. Coffee — can do? Then I had better get in to the office." Turning and gesturing to his vehicle, he went on, "There's a pig in the back there, and it's been on the road, getting here, too long." But as he rounded the bonnet to collect his briefcase and files from the front seat, leaving his suitcase propped up in there for Kaisi to bring in, he thought darkly, that pig, sure, but she's the least of my worries at this juncture, that goes without saying. I'm confronted by events much more distracting and disturbing than the safe delivery of one live pig — or even the mess I've made of my car — about which I have to see David as soon as I can. I only hope he's here, not off on safari miles away.

Salim responded, "Yes, bwana, we heard about the pig as well." Following which, Kaisi with him, he went round the back of the government vehicle to have a look at it; was now peering in at the crate before retreating quickly, muttering disgustedly and throwing up his hands, "Ugh, *chafu sana*!" — dirty creature!

"Best to leave it where it is," Benning said over his shoulder. "I'll get rid of it today with any luck," and he mounted the steps to his veranda.

Salim followed, saying, "Coffee, bwana, yes, two minutes." Asking also, "Breakfast? You had your breakfast at Mtina? All ready, if you like?"

"No, no need, thank you," Benning said. "A mug of coffee, *baba*, please, that'll do. I'll be in the living room." Closing the sliding french door beind him, he crossed the tiled floor to a government-issue armchair and sat himself down, his briefcase on his lap, his files on the low locally-made table beside him. He put his head back and closed his eyes a second or two, reminded all at once that he was seriously short of sleep, before sitting forward again. He didn't open his briefcase to get out the mail he'd brought up with him from Lindi but remained staring, his glance caught and held by the big framed studio portrait, a head and shoulders, of his girl Elizabeth, which she had given him a few days prior to his departure from London, and which now hung by itself on the otherwise bare whitewashed wall facing him. Its ambience coolly silent, rather empty at this hour, with the curtains partly drawn and mid-morning sunlight cutting a swathe of brilliance across the room, she was there for him in all but reality, greeting him in return. Smiling her courtesan's grin, and showing her perfect teeth, her eyes reached out to him, promising him the world, her companionship, her slim and delectable body. All of a sudden he wanted her desperately, his manhood stirring and hardening up at the thought; found it impossible to contemplate, let alone accept, another six months or so of enforced celibacy and deprivation. Because, in fact, they had not slept together as yet — she had refused him that, adamantly, from the outset. It hadn't mattered so much back home, because she had given him everything else, freely and often, her breasts, moulded butt and welcoming thighs, what lay between as well, to kiss and play around with, while she availed herself avidly of his physical perfection in exchange, his male equipment and ardour, with mouth, teeth and strong enfolding hands. That had been enough to keep him hers, if only barely assuaged, *then*. But not now. Sometimes now it all became too much for him and he masturbated, obtaining thereby at least some temporary relief, though sickening himself in the process, and he fantasized in the night about nubile, submissive African girls, like La'ali, any number of whom, in his position, were his for the taking, and not necessarily for payment. But he wasn't going down that road, as more than a few of his kind had always done; no, he was utterly determined not to, for the sake, essentially, of loyalty to his betrothed and the job he sought to do to the best of his ability. He had come this far, with only a few more months to go, without succumbing to that particular temptation, thank God.

Locked away in his bedroom he had a dozen postcard-sized and blatantly revealing snaps of the girl shortly to become Elizabeth Benning — which, laughing and excited, she'd encouraged him to take of her and he'd had developed on the quiet. He rose to his feet again, his movements a little clumsy with lust remembered; put his briefcase down, then went through into the next room, where he slept and indulged in the more lurid of his dreams.

There, Kaisi had dumped his suitcase on the wide single bed, long since neatly made up with clean sheets and a pillow-case, a single cellular blanket, but he left his case where it was for unpacking later and went straight to his bedside table, getting out keys on the way, and unlocked its only drawer. The snaps had been taken in full afternoon sunlight, in a woodland glade in rural Wales, where the two of them had gone hiking together one long weekend two summers ago, based in separate rooms in a small hotel in a nearby market-town. At the height of their yearning for one another and, that day, almost speechless at first, dazed by ravening desire held grudgingly in check, she had stripped off by a stream, waded in — the sun-warmed water only reaching to her knees — and then turned, stretched, laved and caressed herself in full view, and he no more than three yards away. So, quickly, knowing she wasn't averse, he'd found her camera, a Brownie, with a new film inserted in it that morning and, while she thought up new poses, more sexy, more suggestive than on any previous occasion, he snapped her, calling out to her to wait, hold it there, until he'd used up the whole film. After which, trembling and exhilarated, they'd lain together — he by this time as naked as she — and continued their foreplay, both lovingly and with abandon, for nigh on twenty minutes. But even then, she'd retained just sufficient self-control not to permit him to violate her virginity — which he'd believed that, at long last, she expected him to do — and cuffed him hard, wriggled out from under him when, close to bursting point, he was all urgency and in position to penetrate her. Though wet, swollen and ready for him herself she had screamed at him to stop, *please, let her go*, and back off. Which he'd done, because he was incapable of rape, but at once grabbed and lifted her and buried his face in her crotch. After that, spent — and she apologetic and in tears — they had lain together again, bodies entwined; kissed and caressed one another consolingly, until they recovered some semblance of composure. Then he'd sat up beside her, looking down the length of her depilated body, her flush slowly receding, and called her a selfish bitch, but without really meaning it, because it was a distortion of the truth, and as soon as she became quite certain of that, she calmed down and hesitantly reached out for him once more.

But it had hurt him in a complex almost indefinable way, that time, the closest they'd ever come. Not that he didn't accept — had done from the outset — that in deference to parental admonishment, religious teaching and feminine logic, she wasn't going all the way with him before marriage; he did. He saw she was setting him the ultimate test of his love for her and devotion, but that time especially had made the last eighteen months in Africa desperately difficult sometimes when the rutting mood was on him and had him by the balls and throat. In a way he loved and respected her more for the restraint she'd imposed upon him in defiance of her own obvious sexual hunger; at the same time, in retrospect, it had made him rue what he took to be his own lack of the requisite persuasive skills, dominant male intransigence, and — more relevantly — experience, in permitting her to get away with it. In Germany, on National Service, a couple of older and complacent wives had singled him out and allowed him to have sex with them when they felt inclined; a couple of *fräuleins* on the make had targeted him and given him a certain brittle confidence, but that was all. Elizabeth was different — there was a clearly envisaged and beckoning future at stake — yes, he knew that. Still —

"*Kahawa*, bwana," Salim called, from the veranda, breaking into his reverie, and swiftly he put his stills of the promised land of he and she away again in their drawer. They were compelling reminders of a personal chimera which had sustained and driven him, on top of other objectives originally of even greater importance, to work sixteen hours a day, when necessary and put the talents and convictions he'd inherited and grown up with on the line; begin building a worthwhile and rewarding career abroad, and by so doing prove himself worthy of her. But six months longer, not one week less, stretched before him and, increasingly these days, it seemed a *very* long time. Frowning and shaking his head in sudden anguish, he swung round and made his way back through to the sitting-room.

Salim awaited him. A good man. Benning was lucky to have him, and knew it. He was a greying, wiry retainer of forty-five years or so, who had served faithfully and honestly one DC or DO after another at Langoro for more than fifteen years, having started as a garden-*toto* even further back. He had learned to tolerate his employers' sometimes unfathomable moods and various idiosyncracies, befriended them and seen to their needs solicitously when either badly hungover or unwell. These days he had a much younger wife and two small children, a good house and a bit of land on the outskirts of town leading, by this time, to a place among the elders and other serious men at communal gatherings and *barazas*. He had been educated at the local madrassa and was able to read and write Swahili in either European or Arabic script, and had Arab blood in his ancestry — as did many in Langoro District, the result of Arab slaver intrusions in the last century — was of medium height and had the eyes and air of a man at one and basically content with his lot and the life he'd made for himself. He was also an excellent plain cook and, on safari, not one to be taken lightly by backwoods *watu* or anyone else, which had proved a boon to all concerned often enough. To Benning, who paid him well by Langoro standards and to the day on the first of the month, he was indeed indispensible, and the young DO only hoped that if he and Elizabeth returned to Langoro after his coming leave, Salim would still be around waiting for him. His girl, his future wife, was bound to like him; he was as confident of that as he could possibly be.

Now, in the sitting-room, while Benning allowed his coffee to cool, the two of them discussed household requirements — flour, sugar, Harpic, washing powder — to be obtained from the local *dukas* on account. Benning scribbled out, signed and dated a chit armed with which Kaisi could go down into town with his basket and bring back everything needed. Then, with a sense of urgency riding him hard now to get in and see David Morgan and pass on to his superior, and obtain his reaction to, the extraordinary, shocking and bewildering story he had to tell, and also get rid of that pig into hands better able to look after it than his own, he downed his coffee and got to his feet. He confirmerd with Salim lunch at 1.30 as usual and went out to the station Land Rover.

★ ★ ★

In order to enter the District Office — a redbrick building — from the main road, at the side of which Benning left his vehicle, you crossed a broad paved courtyard with the tax-collection office (staffed by long-serving locals) on the left, the Courtroom behind it, and Accounts on the right, a highly competent Nyasa called James Chitembo — little elephant — in charge. Ahead was the veranda where the Messengers, trusted men, in their khaki uniforms took their ease on benches when not otherwise employed, and people sat to await their turn before the offices, left, of the filing clerks and typists, on the right the DO's sanctum. Through that you went in, if you had business with him, reports to make, or an important case to bring a Messenger took you through to see the ultimate authority over an area of villages, broad plains, near-desert, jungle and bush stretching from the boundaries of Southern Highlands Province far to the north to the banks of the great Rovuma river sixty-five miles to the south, the DC. The present incumbent a South African, 32-years-old, a man of culture and earned academic distinction (Michaelhouse and Witwatersrand) who, after the best part of a decade in Dar and Dodoma had put in for and got a posting to a bush station to broaden his experience, and had taken over at Langoro almost a year before. A quiet reserved man, of medium height and compactly built, always impeccably dressed, he displayed a natural courtesy and politeness to all and sundry which tended to mask a meticulous attention to detail plus a steely resolve to ensure that his district should advance — not always in exact keeping with government policy as laid down by the capital — during the time of his stewardship there. By this time Africans of the better sort, and they were the vast majority, from hereditary tribal chiefs to the lowliest contract labourer, regarded him with feelings little short of awe, not least because he was an inveterate walker. He loved it and, casting a perceptive and no-nonsense eye over all that was going on around him, was liable to turn up on their doorsteps without warning, even in the remotest of areas, the senior Messenger at his side, and talk, listen, explain and cajole. The result was that, after his departure, and often before, things got done, bridges repaired, taxes collected, crops more speedily harvested, miscreants arrested, and so on, because, who knew, it was quite likely he'd turn up again to check on progress made. And if he wasn't satisfied, then a village could find itself regarded with extreme disfavour — plainly expressed — and the heads of government-sponsored, and paid, *jumbes* and other local dignitaries could sometimes indeed roll. Of course he and John Benning could not be everywhere at once and things went on behind their backs which were more in conformity with ancient, often pagan, practice than with the law and recent enlightenment. That said, with Benning's unstinted and hard-working support which complemented his own hundred per cent commitment, David Morgan ran a functioning and, on the whole, contented district which did much credit to an often overstretched and under-funded colonial administration in an African country of little natural wealth.

So now, having learnt that David was in fact in his office, John Benning entered his own, walked through and came to a halt in David Morgan's open doorway. But David had people with him, the uniformed police sergeant, Shabani, plus two elderly Africans in headcloths, belted white *khansus*, jackets and sandals, one of whom he recognized as a headman from the Portuguese border, on the Rovuma. So when David looked across and noticed him, Benning merely raised a hand in greeting, nodded and withdrew to wait for his superior officer to be free. Thought how best to report those indefensible and harrowing events in the early hours so that David should be left in no doubt at all that he had been witness to the scenes he described. It worried him a little. For all that by this time David trusted him and would undoubtedly believe him, he might not be able to convey the full, sickening reality of the brutal treatment meted out to that young nun at Mtina last night, so that the DC might decide it was none of their business, not yet at least, that it was almost certainly an isolated incident, and that until further proof of malpractice at the mission came to light — or they were called in — their best course might be not to get involved. To let the mission, whose reputation under Mother Livia's rule was nothing less than excellent, sort out whatever problem it was they had in their own way. Yes, well, John Benning thought, if that was what David Morgan decided was for the best, at any rate for the moment, he'd have to go along with it. But he wouldn't like it, no, because those scenes in the night which he now lived through again in all their cruel and distressing ambiguity in his memory and in which he felt personally involved, more especially in deference to a nagging but deepening sense of personal guilt, seemed to him evidence of circumstances so —

Beyond the doorway facing him but out of sight, he heard Sergeant Shabani stamp to attention on the concrete floor before the DC's desk. Then the sergeant escorted the two *jumbes* — looking a bit chastened — through the doorway, across his office, and away out on to the veranda. Immediately he straightened up, grabbed his briefcase and crossed to David's door and seeing David awaiting him, hands clasped on his blotter, went straight in.

It was a big room with lots of floorspace, uncarpeted, windows facing him and to his left. On the wall between those, the framed Annigoni portrait of the young queen and below her, David's desk, a proper one with drawers. David was smiling in his narrow-eyed tight-lipped way, not a hair of his immaculately barbered blond hair out of place; his thin line of moustache barely visible.

"Hullo, how was Lindi?" he asked, sitting back in his chair. "You had a good time? Very sorry about the car. Can it be fixed?"

"Don't think so," John Benning said sadly, and shook his head; adding, "Thank you for sending Joseph out this morning, he's working on it now but I don't have a great deal of hope, quite honestly." He sat down on one of the two upright chairs across the desk from his DC, laid his briefcase on its side on the desk and went on, "A moment's carelessness, dammit, in the dark, that's all it took." He leaned forward and opened his briefcase and took out the mail and then sorted through it on his lap. Among a stack of bumf which he'd take along to the filing clerks in due course, were two airmail letters for David and one for his wife, a couple of tightly rolled magazines or circulars addressed to them both; two other big white envelopes addressed to D. Morgan, DC Langoro, their contents almost certainly, therefore, confidential. These, with the personal mail, he passed across to David, who didn't look at them for the moment but laid them down to one side, continuing his considering appraisal of the young man before him, with whom, over eleven months, he had established a friendly and productive working relationship. It was vitally important in an isolated district such as this, because in their approach to the job, and to some extent under his tutelage, it was of no little importance that the qualities and attributes they individually possessed supplemented one another's; the younger man's idealistic and extrovert, his own altruistic, yes, maybe, but kept in check by a certain cynicism and natural reserve. Both were thoughtful and intelligent men, with the ambition and abilities to do well and go far in the Service, and if sometimes John Benning's enthusiasms and paucity of experience led him to make mistakes, well, that was youth, and he, David Morgan, was on hand to have a quiet word, if needed. However, at this moment, John looked both tired out, having made the most of the fleshpots of Lindi, no doubt, during his few days of local leave, but, from his eyes and a certain diffidence in his manner, also worried. About his car? Yes, that probably. But perhaps about something else as well. To do with his girl back home? There was always that in the background, and the sooner the boy was married, David thought, and his girl safely out here with him, the better for everyone concerned.

Leaning back in his chair but looking aside, and frowning a little, John Benning said quietly, "I've something to tell you and, if I hadn't seen it with my own eyes, out at Mtina last night, I'd find it very hard to believe."

"Yes?" David said.

"You know I brought a couple of nuns back to the mission from Masasi, Mother Livia and a younger one —"

"Mm, you mentioned it in your note."

"They were very good to me, yesterday evening. I had a slap-up meal and they let me sleep in the rondavel they keep for the Father who visits them."

"I remember it, I think," David said.

"I should explain," Benning said, sitting forward again, "that the young nun — Sister Carmela — I gave a lift to yesterday along with Mother Livia, didn't appear too well in the car on the way back, and she didn't join the others at supper. On top of that I got a strong impression that Mother Livia wasn't exactly pleased with her for some reason which was never revealed."

"I'm with you. Go on."

"Well, something woke me in the night, and . . . and I took a look outside. It was around two o'clock and there were lamps lit in the church the other end of the mission compound. I . . . I was wide awake by that time, and — quietly — I thought I'd go over and see what might be going on, which I did. In case there was some problem and I might be able to help, you understand?"

"And was there?"

"They were *scourging* her, David," John Benning said, his voice rising a little for all his efforts to control it. "Carmela. I looked in through the window by the church door, and she was standing before the altar at the far end, stripped to the waist, and behind her was Mother Livia with a *kiboko* in her hand, which she'd obviously been using because the girl's back and shoulders were striped with the lines of a savage whipping. There was a lot of blood."

Slowly David sat back in his chair, blinked, shook his head and drew breath. Eventually he said, "You're sure about this? You actually saw —?"

"*Yes!*" John Benning said, nodding vehemently. "I watched, you see. I couldn't tear my eyes away. When the whipping they were giving her began again, it didn't stop until Sister Carmela collapsed." He looked down and swallowed, overcome suddenly by choking emotion, but managed, softly, "It was *horrible*, believe me, and the other nuns — you know, the Irish ones? — they were sitting nearby on a bench, and urging Mother Livia on. Also" — he paused fractionally — "something else." He gathered himself and faced his superior officer again. "Something else even more deplorable and incredible, I think. Carmela — She *wanted* them to do it. She was begging, at one point, she actually *begged* Mother Livia not to let up but go on laying into her as if she had the punishment coming and welcomed it as no more than she *deserved*!"

"You? You didn't call out or try to interfere?" David asked.

"No," John said. And at once confessed, though he hadn't intended to, "I should have done, I know I should, but — but it floored me completely, what I was seeing, I suppose, and . . . and I'd no idea what to do for the best, I have to say." He grimaced and hung his head a little in contrition. "So, after a while, when it was all over and the girl could take no more, I slipped away and returned to my rondavel. Then" — he looked up again — "this morning," he concluded, "I had some breakfast in the refectory on my own and, as soon as Joseph arrived, I took my leave of Mother Livia who was in her office by that time, and came back here. To report to you. I thought I had to do that, before anything else."

David nodded in acknowledgment and agreement. Slowly, giving himself time to think, he reached across his desk for his pack of cigarettes; extracted and lit one, then smoked for a few moments in silence, while John Benning waited uncomfortably. A couple of things at any rate to be thankful for, he thought. One, that it was surely the case that David believed him; didn't attribute the extraordinary story he'd had to tell to a touch of the sun, bush-fever or anything of the kind and, while he'd counted on that, it was reassuring, nevertheless, to have it confirmed. Secondly, that David didn't seem inclined to interrogate him further about the barely justifiable sin of omission which he was more than ever convinced he'd committed, in relation to that girl at the climax of those early hours. Thanks be for that as well, though he himself was never likely to find his part wholly acceptable. Behind him, someone appeared at the doorway of the DC's office — clerk or Messenger, very probably — and David looked across and made a small discouraging gesture with his hand.

Seconds later, sitting forward again, he said, "Those nuns, they belong to an offshoot of the Benedictines, called the Dekanian, but I don't know a whole lot about them, that's the truth."

"Me neither," Benning said.

"Could be that, under their rules, the scourging you witnessed is some sort of ultimate deterrent they allow, in exceptional circumstances."

"That occurred to me too," Benning agreed.

"Still, even if it is, it's not permissable — it's medieval — and not to be tolerated in this day and age." David Morgan looked away, and went on, thinking out loud, "They do good work out at Mtina, no doubt about that. At least I've never heard anything against them. In fact, with Mother Livia in charge their involvement in village and community life seems to be wholly beneficial; and that their work is mostly taken up with giving *girls* a better education, in a Muslim area, has to be a good thing."

"Yes, surely," John Benning said.

"So, all right," David said, the next step he should take becoming clear in his mind, "why don't you leave this with me for the time being, and not a whisper to anyone else about what you've told me, all right? I'll keep you informed, I promise you, when I come up with any sort of decision on how best to tackle it. Their visiting Father — Father Simon — was through here while you were down in Lindi, going on to Mingida. I happened to see him and he said he'd be returning to the coast tomorrow but spending a night in Langoro on his way back. So I may well have a word. He's not averse to a beer, I think, so I'll probably invite him up to the house —"

"Why not?" John Benning said.

"And you," David said, looking up and smiling again. "Not too weary? If not, I've a job for you, if you're feeling up to it?"

"No, heck, I'm fine," John said. "Just, I've still got one pig in the back of the car and I thought I'd get her out to Namwea as soon as I can — this afternoon, if that's all right?"

"I'd forgotten the pig — yes, of course, you do that," David said. "Mick" — referring to the Agricultural Officer — "is somewhere out there already. But as soon as you've dealt with that, get on down to Sinyanga, and spend a couple of days there."

"What's the problem?" Benning asked.

"Elephant," David said. "And the Game Scouts report minimal co-operation from the local *jumbes* in driving the herd away."

"Funny," Benning said.

"Yes, it is. So a bit of back-up from us might start things moving."

"Right," Benning said, getting to his feet. "I'll go home now and collect my gear, have a bite to eat, and then get off. May I take Nussoula with me?"

"As you wish," David said. Adding, "And while you're out at Sinyanga have a look at the new school they're building at Koroka. See they're doing it to plan, pay the *fundis*, and chivvy them along a bit."

"Will do," John Benning said, picking up his briefcase in preparation to depart. However, he'd remembered something, and said, "One difficulty only: Joseph, out at Mtina. I promised to go out this evening and bring him back."

"Don't worry about it," David said at once. "I'll send Mustafa for him in my car after work. I'll take care of it." Mustafa, David's houseboy, had been a KAR driver in Ceylon and on the Burmese border during the war, and the DC had trusted him with his own vehicle on numerous occasions in the past.

"Fine then, thank you," John said and, turning away, he headed for the door. But he halted there again for a moment, looking round. Seeing David still watching him though, he decided that to say anything further served no purpose at this stage, so he raised a hand in parting and went out. In sending him off on safari so soon after his return from leave, David might prefer not to have him around at District HQ when he had a meeting with the Father, had crossed his mind. But, if so, it was probably for the best. He only hoped that their discussion might lead to some sort of accommodation between government and mission which — if that was what David was aiming at — could avoid serious and disruptive upheaval, while ensuring that the events of the previous night should under no circumstances be repeated, ever.

CHAPTER FIVE

As the sun went down over mango and jackfruit trees and the scattered roofs of village huts at Sinyanga, he sat at a table on the dais of the red-brick and thatched-roof *baraza* — the local courthouse and meeting-hall — which served a wide area round about. He would sleep in the storeroom at the back, and young men had dug him a latrine nearby ringing it with a circular and shoulder-high wall of plaited palm-frond, to give him privacy. But he was by no means at ease, thinking, while sipping from a big glass of freshly squeezed and sweetened limejuice, gin and water at his elbow, awaiting supper.

He, Salim, and the Messenger called Nussoula — a big man of ample girth to be reckoned with, whom he always liked to have with him on safari and was by this time very close to being a personal friend — had made it out to Namwea, the Agricultural Station by the main road, around 3.30, where, amid much excitement, the poor ill-used sow, obviously in a fairly woeful state by then, had been unloaded and immediately released into the luxurious sty prepared in readiness for her. Up till that time he and the two men with him had had a cramped and uncomfortable time of it but, after being refreshed with as many mugs of tea as they could drink while the back of their *gari* was being cleaned out and allowed to dry, and they set out again, their lot was much improved.

It was forty miles across the *jangwa*, southwards, to Sinyanga, the dirt road, towards the end of the dry season, in very reasonable condition, and they'd got in just before six. While Salim organized his sleeping quarters, cooking facilities and the rest, he'd greeted and been welcomed by the village elders, thanking them for the presents of a chicken and a ripe papaya they'd brought with them, then sent Nussoula off to summon the senior Game Scout and announce that he proposed to hold a meeting first thing in the morning about elephant and crop protection which all village dignitaries and others from nearby villages were requested, more like *ordered*, to attend. He'd then sat down with the top Game Scout, who hadn't been far away, and received his report which — the man being a foreigner in these parts and an old growler by nature — consisted mostly of a fairly disparaging assessment of the level of intelligence, coupled with a general disinclination to lift a finger on their own behalf, of the local people and their so-called leaders hereabouts.

So, all right, John Benning said, before sending the old warrior away, thinking there had to be more to it than so far met the eye. They'd all have a chance to talk the matter over and air their views in the morning, after which, he hoped and expected, a more helpful attitude might reasonably be forthcoming. Eventually, and knowing his way around the village, which was a big one, from previous visits, he'd strolled off in the direction of the tree-shadowed open space which was the village's market square, to show his face, greeting and being greeted by men returning home from the fields; women, their young children around them, pounding maize in giant pestles beside their open doorways, before he ended up at one of the two Indian *dukas*, built of split axed timber and rusty corrugated iron. There he bought a couple of tins of condensed milk and sat down briefly at the counter to take a cup of tea while exchanging general and family news with the owner: none of it, as it turned out, of more than passing interest or concern to him.

Now, back at the *baraza* and while he waited for night to fall, Salim to bring him a lamp, a *debe* of water to wash and supper, he felt tired to the bone. It had been a long, long day after the night before, and those which had preceded it, beginning at Mtina in early morning and closing with the coming of darkness over a hundred miles away. And while he smoked and downed his gin, he thought about women, more particularly a girl. Not the one soon to become his bride, but the other one, as he'd last seen her in Mother Livia's office that morning, who had seemed to be seeking for his understanding and compassion. Certainly she had *that* — had, perhaps, been trying to reveal herself to him, both angrily, defiantly, and with a plea for mercy. *She!* She *called* to him — her demeanour, her dark Latin good looks, the provocation in her eyes and lithe inviting body so cruelly and hauntingly exposed in all its half-naked female symmetry while enduring the vicious chastisement inflicted upon it but a few hours before in a way which stimulated his imagination, aroused in him the most basic of carnal thoughts, of which he was ashamed, but also protective instincts, which he found it impossible to dismiss out of hand. He couldn't get it out of his head that she'd been trying to say she wanted to speak to him alone, and confess the agonies of doubt which tormented her — was that it? — needed his sympathy, or her life would be insufferable and she would descend even further into hell, her pain so destructive that she might as well end it. Christ, too fanciful by a wide margin, he told himself: she was a nun, and presumably, therefore, immune to such distracted yearnings and personal disorientation — wasn't she? Not only wrong, but muddled and juvenile thinking on his part, also pointless speculation of the naïvest kind. Nonetheless his feelings about her, and for her, simply refused to go away. Doubtless his sense of guilt over those scenes, as he'd permitted them to develop during the hours of darkness, made it more difficult for him, actually impossible, to put her right out of his mind, as he knew he should. He'd better start learning to live with it, somehow, he supposed.

Night suddenly, and with it the arrival of Salim with a pressure lamp which he hung on a wire from a roofbeam and turned up the mantle so that the shadowy confines of the *baraza* before him — the red-brick pillars surrounding it, the supporting timbers and thatch above the concrete floor — were revealed once again. In five minutes, Salim said, a boy would bring him water and, after that, as soon as the bwana was ready, supper would follow. Out back they'd been having a bit of trouble with the *kuni* — the firewood — he explained apologetically, but finally they'd got it burning properly, at last. Didn't matter, he wasn't in any hurry, Benning said, and Salim departed again.

To pass the time he thought he'd have a second drink; he needed it, he suspected, and anyway he was still thirsty. So he got up, took down the lamp, grabbed his empty glass, and went inside to the long narrow room in which he would sleep. There, on one of the several benches stacked against the wall, close to his made-up camp-bed, Salim had laid out his towel, soap and teeth things, an enamel basin and mug, a now partly depleted jug of drinking water, a jam jar containing sugar, plus, on a saucer, the remaining half of a fresh-cut lime. Beside that stood the bottle of Gordon's which, being colourless, was the tipple he tended to favour on safari. All Europeans, including the district's present DO, partook of strong liquor of one sort or another — the better ones only after the day's work was over. It was, of course, common knowledge if not always true but, in Benning's opinion, there was no need to advertise the fact to watching eyes which, in a bush village such as this one, were often upon him whether he was aware of it or not.

When he left his room again, refilled glass in hand, and returned to his place at table, it was to find Nussoula awaiting him. Dressed now in a loose white *kansu* and his head swathed in a turban, the big man had doubtless come to take his leave of him for the night before returning to whatever billet the village elders had prepared for his use. A highly comfortable one, no doubt, with excellent food provided, a boy to serve him and, if requested, a woman, because, like others, these villagers surely believed that if they kept the DOs, or other important government officials' minions on side, then their various causes were likely to proceed a lot more smoothly, and to their advantage, than if they didn't bother. That back in his home village on the Rovuma Nussoula had three wives and umpteen children — with another on the way — was no concern of Benning's, his Messenger's perks while out on safari far better not enquired into too closely. So long as his work remained irreproachable — as it had always — so long as no question of outright bribery ever raised its head, then what Nussoula's private arrangements might amount to in this village or that, such as he knew of them, only tended to inspire in him no little admiration and respect!

After hanging up the lamp again, above him and to one side, giving them plenty of light, he resumed his seat and looked up, saying, "You're going now, *baba* — no problems?"

"No, bwana, they know me here."

"Good," Benning said. Then, seriously, "This business of the elephant. Before we hold our meeting with everyone in the morning, see if you can find out why these people are being so" — he gestured, searching for the right word — "so obstructive."

"I know why, bwana. Already I know that."

"You do? Why then?"

"*Dawa*, bwana," Nussoula said.

"*Dawa*?" Benning repeated softly, in surprise. "In what way, *dawa*?" Sorcery: the old ways, the old beliefs, fears, the old power which must be propitiated. In this case?

Nussoula turned and looked out into the night in a south-easterly direction, far beyond the village of Sinyanga. Few Africans, very few indeed, would so much as hint at, let alone admit, to a European what *dawa*, its practice and effects meant to them, for fear of ridicule, among other things. But Nussoula was one, and in that way Benning knew himself both privileged and trusted. His Messenger's reasons for being thus open with him were nothing if not laudable, he thought, and came down to the basic premise that the man did not like it, *dawa*, and he owed allegiance to the white officers he served, to whom *dawa* was the past. He was big enough to resolve that, if they weren't afraid of it, then neither was he. More power to him; it took courage and a clear-eyed, if cynical, perception of his own peoples' failings, no doubt of that.

"The villages out there," Nussoula said, making a face, "them. This herd of elephant crossed the Rovuma further up and came here. *Here* is where it is causing trouble, also near Koroka and round there. So, those distant villages say, let them stay in these parts, those elephant, and not be turned in our direction. A week and more ago they made strong "medicine", brought it and left it where the Koroka and Sinyanga people would find it, which they did. And they know what it means, that those elephant, if they leave here and go *that* way, as they are likely to do, then very bad trouble will follow, worse than elephant, for everyone here. Those other villages, you understand, their medicine is more powerful than anything these people have. That is the reputation they have built up over many many years, so the people of Sinyanga are very anxious not to offend them, so keep quiet and do nothing."

Slowly Benning sat back in his chair, frowning and nodding thoughtfully; took a long pull at his gin while he absorbed what he'd been told; knowing he was dead beat, but that this was vitally important because it was harvest-time, and if the harvest around Sinyanga was ruined —

Eventually he asked, "So, *baba*, what do *you* suggest? Is there a way out of this that I can put to the people tomorrow, in the hope it may allay their fears and get them to change their minds?"

"One way, maybe, bwana," Nussoula said at once. He paused briefly, then spoke very seriously. "You say nothing about *dawa*, of course, but at the meeting which the three Game Scouts must be summoned to attend, you speak out and say forcefully so that the elders hear you, believe you and afterwards spread the word, that you are ordering those Game Scouts, with the people's help, to drive that herd away from here in a westerly direction" — he turned and pointed — "then keep after them to see the herd stays clear of those other villages and their crops, and heads off into the bush where very few people live. Also that never mind any other work they may have at this time, they have instructions to shadow that herd and drive it before them, for two-three weeks if necessary, until it crosses the Rovuma again and we hope, doesn't come back this side any more this year."

"You think that might do it?" Benning asked.

"Yes, I don't see why not," Nussoula said. "These people here, they hate to see the destruction of their crops — all their hard work over many months going to waste. They fear famine and hardship after the turn of the year, so if the greater fear they have, of *dawa*, is removed" — Nussoula shrugged — and concluded, "it's worth a try, I think. Provided the Game Scouts have their orders, and no one interferes, as soon as the people have thought it over, their attitude may well change and they'll give the Game Scouts all the support they need to get the job done."

Thinking it through, Benning said, "And *my* job will be to see that no bigshot Game *Ranger*, arriving in Langoro from Lindi or Mingida, sticks his nose in and countermands those instructions before the work is properly finished."

"Right, bwana," Nussoula said. "Yes, that's it, and you should swear a solemn oath, before the people, that you will keep your word."

After a few moments, Benning nodded and said slowly, "All right then, yes, I agree. Let's do it that way and hope for the best." And he added, "You get off now, *baba*, and take your food. Your advice seems very good to me and I thank you for it."

"*Si kitu*" — It's nothing — "bwana," the big Messenger said and, seeing a boy weighed down with a steaming *debe* of water approaching around the side of the building, he salaamed and took his leave, disappearing shortly into the night.

There was one thought only in Benning's mind as, rising to his feet and taking down the lamp, he ushered the boy through into his sleeping quarters, then thanked and dismissed him; shrugged off his shirt prior to cleaning up a bit; after that eat the food prepared for him and perhaps read for half an hour before hitting the sack. That Nussoula was an excellent example of the men, the good men — and there were not a few of them, often of little education but of the people — who had chosen to throw in their lot with the *wazungu* — the white men — not only for the pay and perks, the position of local influence, but because they held steadfastly to the opinion that they knew the way forward to a better future for their country in a changing world. Given any sort of leadership from men of a different race who would pay heed to their priorities and were prepared to work tirelessly to that end, they were the ones who actually enabled the administration to leave its mark on the ground and do so with reasonable efficiency and benevolence. Without them the whole thing was little better than a charade. He only prayed that when the time came for his people to pull out of this part of Africa, and, as the writing was already on the wall, that time couldn't be delayed for many more years, such men would not end up despised and disillusioned and called collaborators because the part they'd played had in fact been of inestimable worth.

⋆ ⋆ ⋆

Father Simon was fifty-two years old, but looked older, and had once been a scholar. Impelled by his conscience he had allowed himself to be wrenched from the groves of academe at the beginning of the war and, by the end of it, had made acting half-colonel in a frontline regiment, with an MC and bar, acquired in Sicily and on the Burmese border. He was though — despite taking holy orders shortly after demobilization — a broken man as a result of his experiences. Under his white thatch of hair, behind the mask of reserved good fellowship he showed to the world, he was a man who believed in nothing any longer, paid little more than lip-service to the Saviour he called his own, and loathed the world-weariness which dogged his footsteps. Through connections in the wider church he had got himself sent out to Africa in an attempt at personal rehabilitation, since there he might do more good than further harm, and asked only for a quiet life while he fulfilled the tasks allotted to him. He was often on the move, which he quietly enjoyed, the solitude, harsh landscape, and being beyond anyone's reproach from Mission HQ at Lindi all the way to Mingida, visiting the four mission stations in his pastoral care, where he was made welcome and he listened but, by this time, not a great deal was expected of him. He did his best, of course, but, well, such influence as he'd ever had was a thing of the past. He was a straight, good man but tired of himself and life.

He drove up through the town to the DC's bungalow at Langoro around 5.30 in the late afternoon; only the second time he'd been invited there since David

Morgan's takeover a year or so ago. He wondered why; something had surely come up, and it could prove of passing interest, you never knew. He only hoped it might not involve too much of a break in his long-established routine, but, of course, all would doubtless shortly be revealed. These government types who had their own agendas and were subject to orders beyond their control, were best kept at arms' length, if that were possible — and it usually was — at all times. However, a glass of ale — as promised in the DC's note — wouldn't come amiss, and he was looking forward to it.

At the top of the steps leading up to the veranda, David Morgan's wife had come out to meet him. A city girl from Melbourne, Australia, whom David had met on leave in Durban, she found life in an isolated bush-station nearly intolerable, was rarely seen and, during the last year, had ceased to bother about what once, surely, had been a striking and dramatic appearance. Of Spanish extraction, she overindulged, both as to liquor (on the quiet) and starchy foods; she had therefore put on weight, her tawny complexion was ruined, she wore no make-up, and her long mane of hair was a mess. None of which, since the departure of their two children south, appeared to bother her one bit, or not sufficiently, anyway, and she presented a narrow-eyed, resentful and unwelcoming face to the world. It was in fact the first time she and Father Simon had ever met, and he was both startled and dismayed. She wore a brocade housecoat, rather too open at the neck, and, in embarrassment the Father looked away.

In her heavy accent she said, gesturing, "Why you don't go in, Father — the sitting-room on your left. The DC's having a wash; soon he'll come and you'll see him in there." Ignoring, perhaps not noticing, the hand he tentatively extended in greeting, she turned and went off along the veranda. He shook his head slightly, eyed her retreating back for a moment, then, as it had been suggested he should, he went inside. When he reached what he took to be the sitting-room doorway, he came to a halt, feeling uncomfortable and uncertain what he should do next. The big lofty room before him wasn't too well lit at this hour of the day, the uncurtained casement windows opening inwards behind fine wiremesh frames. It contained basic government-issue furniture, scattered Persian rugs on the polished floor, a Victorian escritoire and baroque chair and a bar filling one corner. A trio of big framed photos (of the hugh veldt, maybe?) adorned one yellow-ochre wall.

This was all he had time to notice and remember from his previous visit before David Morgan came silently to stand at his shoulder, saying apologetically, "Sorry, Father, please go on in and make yourself comfortable. I was a little late back from the office today. You'll join me in a beer?"

"Thank you, that would be very kind," Father Simon said. Selecting a cushioned armchair facing the window, beyond which lay the shaded veranda and massy trees, outside, he settled down, smoothing his white cassock over his knees. His skinny, bony knees were arthritic, from the high-jungle swampland below Kohima where they'd been pinned down by sniper and mortarfire for weeks. It was painful sometimes but to be accepted with resignation. A cigarette, though, to ease his nerves, he could use one now and hoped the DC might offer.

He did, and he lit it for him, after presenting him with a tall ice-cold glass from the kerosene fridge behind the bar, which Father Simon held carefully on his lap until the DC was seated also, opposite, his face in shadow. A neat well-set-up figure of a man, the Father thought, good officer-material, his authority understated but real enough, except that in that way appearances could too often be misleading.

"Your health, Father," David Morgan said, and raised his glass. They both drank, the Father with genuine appreciation: the beer was Tuborg and he hadn't had the pleasure in a while. As he was putting down his glass on the table beside him, David Morgan began, a little awkwardly, "I asked you here not only for the pleasure of seeing you but because I need to speak to you about something." Pausing a moment David looked away, but then went on, "Father, forgive me, but I'm not familiar with the rules of your Order. In particular" — fractionally he paused again to choose his words — "in particular, does it permit physical chastizement in case of error? If a brother or nun transgresses, seriously transgresses . . .?" He didn't finish.

"You're speaking about, what?" Father Simon asked slowly. "Mortification of the flesh inflicted on the transgressor by his superiors or peers? No, it does not permit that, not under any circumstances, not even as a last resort." He added, in curiosity and astonishment, "What has given you this idea that it might, if I may ask? Please be good enough to tell me. Whatever you may have heard, believe me, it can only be a tissue of lies."

"My first reaction too," David Morgan said, easing himself to greater comfort in his chair. "But then I thought I'd better make absolutely certain, hence my invitation for you to call in and see me today. You see, my informant — and I assure you he was badly shaken by what he believed he'd witnessed — was my young DO, John Benning. You've met him, I think. Two nights ago he was out at Mtina. He spent the night there and enjoyed their hospitality, because his car had broken down —"

"And he saw something? Is that what he says?"

"Yes, he did."

"What exactly?"

"One of the young nuns — she was before the altar in the church there, in the middle of the night. She was naked to the waist and was being scourged with a *kiboko* —"

"Nonsense!" Father Simon blurted, sitting forward, his agitation getting the better of him. "He was dreaming, he must have been — your DO — or he's making it up! Perhaps he'd been drinking, or wasn't well? I mean — Who was it, doing the scourging, did he say?"

"Yes. Mother Livia."

"Mother Livia! Not possible, unthinkable! She is a woman of outstanding character and integrity, and held in the highest regard by everyone I know."

"According to John Benning, the girl was urging her on. Even though her back was already cut and bleeding, she was crying out she wanted more."

"God in Heaven," Father Simon said softly, sitting back. "And you, you believe him, your DO, this story of his?"

"I have to, I think," David Morgan said. "Though young and inexperienced, he's never been other than honest with me before, that I know of. If he'd been in any way uncertain of what he'd seen, he'd have said so. Nor, in my hearing, has he ever expressed even a hint of antipathy towards your people or your missions. The reverse, in fact. Up till now I'd formed the opinion that, like myself, he views all you do with nothing but commendation and approval."

"I . . . I don't know what to say," Father Simon murmured and, suddenly, raising his glass again in a shaking hand, he drained it to the last. Patently sweating now, he dabbed at his mouth with a kerchief he took from his sleeve, blinking and looking away.

"Let me fill your glass, Father," David Morgan offered, getting up.

"Very kind, yes, thank you." Father Simon handed it across. And to the DC's back, over his shoulder "You wish me . . . in this case — What is it you wish me to do? Something like this, if it were to come out, or rumour get around —"

"Yes, I agree," David remarked, behind him.

"I mean," Father Simon said throatily, "if an allegation like this were proven, then the authorities — yourself and your superiors — would be bound to close us down, would they not, and our work here would be finished?"

"Yes, without a doubt," David said. Returning from the bar he passed the Father's glass into his waiting hand before sitting down again. "So our best course, perhaps, with your permission, may be to treat this as an isolated incident and by no means proven to have any basis in fact, as yet."

"Yes, all right."

"You will speak to Mother Livia as soon as you can."

"I will indeed. Tomorrow. But if she denies all knowledge —?"

"She may well. But then you will use your authority to take the girl away from her so her back and physical condition can be examined by a qualified doctor and a report submitted."

"But if I take her to Lindi, if I were to do that, and she *has* been abused, then everything will be out in the open straightaway. And that would be a disaster."

"Yes, I appreciate that. So, in the first instance, and as quickly as you can, why don't you bring her back here? To our station doctor here? He's a Goan whom I will swear to secrecy, using *my* authority, before he examines her. Then, after he has seen her, at least you and I will know for sure, one way or the other, and we can decide together on such steps to take as may be necessary."

"Why not, yes, I agree and . . . it's good of you," the Father said. "This has all come as so much of a shock to me. I don't know whether to believe it or not, but yes, what you suggest seems to me as good a way forward as any, for the moment. Thank you."

"It won't be easy, dealing with Mother Livia, I dare say," the DC said.

"No. No, it won't," Father Simon said, his eyes down. "No, indeed, I can't say I'm looking forward to it at all."

"But it must be done, Father," David Morgan said, a certain steel entering his voice. "No delays, no prevarications — you understand that, don't you?"

"Yes, I do, yes," Father Simon said miserably, and stood up, his second beer untouched, to take his leave.

Benning returned from Koroka around 3.30 in the afternoon. Following a great deal of discussion that morning and, on his side, a forceful expression of intent, the issuing of explicit orders to the three Game Scouts had ended in what he hoped would be the successful galvanizing of the villagers of Sinyanga to play their part. Afterwards he had packed the headman of Koroka and four others of that village's leading men, into his car for the five-mile drive to their homes, leaving Nussoula at Sinyanga to keep an eye on things and ensure that the people didn't change their minds as soon as his back was turned.

At Koroka, a widely scattered settlement, he'd been shown the pitiful sight of fields and banana plantations where the errant herd had done its worst. He had commiserated with the owners, then harangued everyone briefly, a second time, to get up off their backsides and help the Game Scouts drive the herd right away, westwards, before stopping for an hour at the site of the new primary school under construction.

There, in the company of the two Nyasa *fundis*, he'd inspected the work done and in progress. The long mud-brick, forest-timber and thatched-roof building was not far off completion. Then, getting out his cashbox, he settled up with both *fundis* and those local labourers whose *kipandes* showed their attendance at work over the past month or so. There were no problems as far as he could see; the work was going forward to a satisfactory standard and on schedule; the *fundis* were reasonably content although eager to finish up and get home to their wives and families so, after making a list of their needs in the way of nails, solignum, the odd replacement tools, and so on, which he promised to despatch on his return to Langoro, he spoke words of encouragement, got back in his vehicle, and had his lunch: cheese sandwiches, a couple of bananas and a flask of tea, put up by Salim. While he was so occupied, a few local people, the headman among them, gathered nearby and, after eating, he sat down with them and listened to what they had to say concerning non-payment of tax because of illness, a boundary dispute, and other parochial matters — and arbitrated as fairly and carefully as he knew how on such evidence as was laid before him, in an endeavour to sort things out both justly and with the minimum of ensuing rancour. Only once did he have to raise his voice and lay down the law when he believed himself lied to, but that was also part of the job and he didn't shirk it.

Well on into the afternoon he left for Sinyanga again with a couple of *totos* in the back along for the ride.

Sitting now at the magistrate's table on the dais in the *baraza* at Sinyanga, a mug of sweet condensed-milk tea at his elbow, he was using the time to write up his notes, which could be turned, if needed, into a detailed report on what had transpired and been agreed at his meeting this morning while all that had gone on remained clear in his mind. Particularly when another department of government and its employees — in this case those attached to Game and Conservation — was involved, the notes could well be required to provide extra back-up, if questions were raised about the administration's interference, and however pressing the occasion, in matters some stickler might consider not strictly subject to their jurisdiction. It was a practice which David Morgan had instigated and insisted upon as soon as he arrived in Langoro, and it had already proved its worth as a calmer of troubled waters in relation to more than one incident in the recent past. There just wasn't time, in an isolated district such as this one, to go through the correct channels in every instance. In any case the DC was the ultimate authority and responsible for the broader picture, was he not? With this John Benning fully agreed, so he penned his notes, struggling sometimes both with memory and exact wording, and setting down his source material which would permit his superior officer to smooth down ruffled feathers which, conceivably, might have to be undertaken at some later date.

But while he did so, drank his tea and occasionally sat back, he was also thinking about something else: that this was the day — probably even around now — when David Morgan would be having his meeting with Father Simon about that frightful and heart-rending event he had witnessed in all its abhorrent brutality out at Mtina two nights ago. He trusted David, without question: both in the matter of taking his word for it, but also to do the right thing, whatever that might be. The trouble was there was more than one way of looking at it. For a start, did he also trust Father Simon, in the same way? No, he didn't. He hardly knew the man but, by repute and on brief personal acquaintance, had found him something of an enigma. A genuine war hero which was, of course, wholly admirable, and a good man, he was almost certainly burnt-dry — a good description — a cypher, and with such scruples as were left to him subject to a general weariness which disempowered him when and if the chips were down. As now, you could say, they were, and the easy option was there for the taking. It might even be the right one, in the circumstances, but was a reprehensible and perhaps cruel solution, nevertheless. Would David Morgan agree with it? Maybe he'd have to in the interest of saving the mission, and allow Mother Livia to continue the good work which she and the others normally did.

Was a cover-up all he could expect and, with it, the desperate plight of that girl — whatever she thought she'd done to deserve punishment — ignored, suppressed, until — what? What would happen to her? He was afraid for her, he knew it: that *she'd* be made the scapegoat, be spirited away and Mother Livia no more than warned in private and permitted to carry on as before. She was a flawed and remorseless woman and that it might be the girl, the victim, who would have to pay didn't sit easily with him, no, not one bit. What would the girl herself want to do now, he wondered, when the threat of everything coming out into the open was revealed, as surely quite soon it would be? How dedicated was she, and how strong in her faith? He had no idea, but felt for her, remembering vividly her eyes and the look she'd given him in Mother Livia's office which caused him, at the very least, to reserve judgment. He remembered also his own inadequacy, with which he was still finding great difficulty in coming to terms and probably never would, that he had stood by and watched her suffer; done nothing, not one single thing, to come to the girl's assistance, whether she liked it or not, and stop it. My God, what had got into him?

It was after he had completed his notes and was reading through them before putting them away in a file that he picked up the sound of a vehicle approaching, a rare sound in these parts. From the pitch and growl of its engine it wasn't a pick-up bringing in stock for the *dukas*, but a Land Rover, its four-wheel-drive sometimes engaged as it negotiated the steep banks of the river between Sinyanga village and the north. And not just any Land Rover, he realized very quickly, *his* Land Rover. He recognized it as soon as it came into view and surely he couldn't be mistaken? In real excitement he got to his feet, scraping back his chair, as the car came nearer along the trail to his left, sometimes hidden by acacia trees. That it really *was* his was confirmed by the arrival of Salim and Nussoula from round the back of the *baraza*, standing waiting, watching it as delightedly and amazedly as he was himself. It was stripped bare, both doors, canopy and supporting struts left behind, only the windscreen in place, but, unquestionably, his own vehicle.

Joseph swung her in a wide turn so that John could see the front mudguard, its panels beaten back into shape, spot-welded with sheet metal and given a preliminary coating of dull-grey primer which contrasted with the darker green of the rest of the vehicle, before drawing up alongside the *baraza* and getting down, a broad grin all over his face. Benning was already there, Salim and Nussoula at his shoulder, to meet him, his hands raised, palms open, in surprise and wonder, his smile matching that of the tough, sturdily built African mechanic before him.

"She's OK? You did it?" he exclaimed. "Joseph, how did you manage it?" And again, "She's all right, she doesn't have to go in for repair?"

"No, bwana, she's fine," Joseph said. "See, I'll show you." And he hunkered down by the realigned front bumper while Benning did the same. Together they knelt on the sand, peering under and up by the front wheel, as Joseph pointed out and explained what he'd done. "Steering-rods no problem," he said, "I straighten them. Shock-absorber mounting more difficult, but I bolt and weld piece of angle-iron to chassis — see there — then bolt mounting back to that. Stronger now than it was before, bwana, has to be, for sure."

Slowly, the light under there not good, Benning ran his eye over the dust-coated repairs which Joseph had effected. Truly they looked good, strong and permanent, and anyway his *gari* had since been driven here over rough roads without mishap, a distance of more than eighty miles. He shook his head in acknowledgment and acceptance.

"Brake cable, fuel pipe not broken," Joseph went on, pointing again. "I re-attach, top up brake fluid. Mudguard easy, bit of panel-beating and welding needed, then this morning I give it a coat of primer at Langoro. Only headlight no good — all smashed, can't do anything about that. We send to Lindi for a new unit which will take a bit of time, but sidelight OK — see? I had a spare one, and it's working all right again."

"Really, Joseph, fantastic," Benning breathed, getting to his feet. And, "I can't thank you enough, truly, you've worked wonders. Come inside, let's have some tea. Would you like something to eat? Will you stay the night? What d'you want to do?"

"Ah, it's all right, bwana," Joseph said. "Salim make me a mug of tea, that would be good, thank you. Then I get back to Langoro before nightfall. I take the station-*gari*, leave yours with you. I filled her up with petrol and there's a four-gallon can in the back."

"If you're sure, then," John said. "If that's what you'd prefer." And he added, "I'll see you at Langoro as soon as I return — day after tomorrow, I expect." Meaning that Joseph had earned, deserved and was destined to receive a substantial reward, almost certainly in cash (which would suit him best) for all the hard work he had put in, not to mention the skill and inventiveness he'd shown, in getting Benning's car back on the road again. Then the two men shook hands once more — Benning repeating his words of gratitude and sincere relief — before Joseph took his leave and he and Salim went off together to disappear round the end of the *baraza*.

Benning and Nussoula, still in uniform, stood — in both cases arms akimbo — contemplating this vehicle, now returned to them, which, in an important and life-enhancing sense, had become theirs over the last ten months, since Benning had bought it. They'd thought they'd lost it, for many weeks at least, but here it was again, restored to them after its accident. To have it in working order once more, so soon, gave their hearts — the young DO's especially, but the big Messenger's almost equally — a definite lift. Freedom, no longer to be dependent on others for transport, the deprivations of which hadn't really sunk in before now, was a bit like an unexpected gift of manna from Heaven. Stepping forward, Benning patted the bonnet of his car affectionately; then continued on, Nussoula at his side — both silent — while they rounded the vehicle, looked in the open back, and went on round to the front where all the damage had been done and, for the most part, put to rights. A couple of coats of matching paint, a new headlight — both readily available from stock in Lindi, so merely a matter of time — were nothing: one big light instead of two, temporarily, of little importance. Back at Langoro the torn canopy could quickly be patched and sewn up by one of the Indian *dukas* there, and anyway he had done without it before, from choice — the doors as well — sometimes for weeks on end. So yes, while there remained a few comparatively minor things which needed attention, they were back in business properly once more and glad of it.

After a moment or two Benning looked round at the man who went most places with him these days, and said seriously, "Mendi tomorrow, *baba*" — a village ten miles to the east of Koroka from where, so Nussoula had reported a half-hour ago, word had been received that the elephant herd had reappeared this very morning and been wreaking havoc and destruction in the vicinity,

"'*diyo*, bwana," Nussoula said, nodding agreement. Then, as seriously and thoughtfully, "If you wish, I send word through to Mendi tonight that you're coming, and that you expect to hear that the Game Scouts have already begun their work of turning the herd back and towards the big river."

"Yes, good," Benning said immediately. "You get off and see that's done. Then take your food early, and get a good night's sleep. We'll be on our way at first light and, who knows, we may be tramping around in the bush all day."

Nodding again, Nussoula salaamed and left at once, marching off purposefully in the direction of the village. The sun was going down now, the shadows lengthening, and Benning went back inside, swinging round for another glance at his *gari* as if to make sure it was still there before resuming his seat and beginning to tidy his papers away into his briefcase. Shortly Joseph appeared outside, gave him a wave, to which he responded, then got into the old station Land Rover and drove off, disappearing along the trail, northwards, among the trees.

Stretching out his legs and crossing his ankles, Benning sat on, thinking. Knowing it made a big difference, having his own vehicle again, plus, with the spare can, a full tank of petrol: with her newer engine she did a lot better than the seven or eight to the gallon which was all the old one managed these days. So tomorrow to Mendi — and, after that? He'd spend the whole day there, if necessary, but, provided all appeared to be going well, the Game Scouts doing their stuff, the locals co-operating, and so on — there'd be little more for him to do in these parts and he might as well get back to Langoro. But why stop there? The more he thought about it, the more he was tempted to go straight on through and out to Mtina, a mere thirty miles further. See what was happening — if anything, yet — about that girl, that young nun, and those around her with whom she worked. Mother Livia, her position — which patently she'd grossly abused — the continued existence of the mission itself, might well depend on what that girl agreed to divulge, or was compelled to under threat. He was the only outsider to have actually witnessed what had taken place, in its gory detail and, apparently, at her behest, so what did *she* feel about it now? Was she recovering? What did she see as the way forward, for herself and everyone else? He could guess, but was he right? Far better to talk to her, if he could, in person and in private: make it plain to her that she wasn't friendless and alone. In a complex but obvious way he owed her that, he thought.

But no, forget it, he told himself, the girl's predicament — whatever that might be and had led to it — wasn't his concern any more and was now in the hands of others. Only, that Father . . . It was an undeniable fact that John Benning mistrusted him and didn't much care for the idea that *his* judgement and participation must play a crucial role.

CHAPTER SIX

That same day, Sister Carmela — or Jeanne Michaela Rawson as she was named on her birth certificate and as she remained in her heart and memory, with all her chequered history behind her — rested a second day in her cell, one of four adjoining, recuperating and gathering her strength, while she consulted the promptings both of her physical intransigence and conscience. Twice during the day, Mother Livia, her genuine concern for her and authority over her equally in evidence, visited her, the first time to examine her wounds and re-dress them, a painful but healing process; the second, in early evening, to talk to her, counsel her and confirm her intentions and state of mind. This was after La'ali had brought her supper of broiled diced kid, sweet potato, unleavened bread and an orange, and she had eaten well. Then she had spent another interlude of time on her knees before her personal prie-dieu, more to seek consolation by doing so than with any expectation of reaching a lasting decision.

But even before Mother Livia's arrival that second time, her decision had been maturing, coming to a head. It was just one of the options open to her, but the only one which made any sense. She needed the world of men, the vividly remembered bodily excitement and euphoria of the male animal within her, ravishing her, the surrender of her body to blind lust and long-drawn-out and exquisite pleasure, leading to the personal domination of one man and the imposition of her will over him, sufficient to make him her slave as she became his. She couldn't do without that, not for ever, the chance and possibility she would get lucky, again, and no amount of flagellation, self-abasement, service to others and submission of the self to higher ideals, was going to change her. For four whole years she had dutifully and eagerly followed the regimen laid down for her; she'd given it her best shot, but now she wanted out. That part of her life was over — had served its purpose, she admitted, but as a lifetime's commitment it was not for her.

In other words, that beating she had begged for and welcomed, passionately and despairingly, two nights ago, hadn't worked. It had merely served, in retrospect — and given her ongoing pain and mounting revulsion — to strengthen her resolve, the other way.

However, by the time Mother Livia put in an appearance that evening, her final decision, to go for it, had not been taken, not quite — because she was a coward at heart, she told herself. Full stop. That and the acknowledged fact that Mtina, the mission, was not a bad environment in which one could aspire to make one's peace with the world and Almighty God. Indeed you could say it was deeply satisfying in relation both to her teaching and her girls if only, in recent days, at a quite different and though diminishing still seriously important level of priority. Yes, true.

The older woman had entered, using her key and bringing a lamp with her because, within the cell, there was little light from outside through the single small, barred window. Initially she tidied Jeanne's supper plates together on the tray at the table; then placed it on the floor and sat down on the lone upright chair beside it. Jeanne stayed where she was, seated on the side of her bed. So far Mother Livia hadn't spoken — merely glanced at her once or twice — but at last she broke the silence.

"How's it feeling, Sister? Is it still hurting you? Shall I look at it again?"

"No need, Mother, thank you," Jeanne said, moving her shoulders a little. "It feels a lot better, I promise you. I'll be right as rain by morning."

"Hardly," Mother Livia said. "You'll have to take it very easily for another day or two, I think." She paused. "And the other matter? You didn't forget to apply the medication they gave you today?"

"No, no, I didn't," — which was the truth. "That's also clearing up pretty well, I'm glad to say."

"Good." Again Mother Livia hesitated. "So, from tomorrow, and taking it very gently at first, you'd like to resume your duties, as before?"

"Yes, I would. You and the others, you've been covering for me with my classes, I know, and I'm very sorry about that."

"It wasn't a problem," Mother Livia said, and looked at her, studying her again.

Jeanne Rawson returned her look, by an effort of will contriving not to drop her eyes. So far she had spoken convincingly — hadn't she? — but with a woman like Mother Livia, the reverse of gullible and with years of experience behind her, it was hard to be quite certain. Of course she would resume her duties on the morrow, as long as she felt well enough, play her part to the full in mission life, but only until such time as it might be possible to make her escape with at least a 50-50 chance of success. At this point, again — and by no means for the first time that day — a picture of that young DO entered her mind, as she had last seen him standing there, fair, rangily built and shy, in Mother Livia's office. She recalled — with a momentary stirring in her gut — the touch and smell of him the day before on that long drive up from Masasi. She coveted him, no question — all that raw male charisma and sexuality — the only personable young male she had actually been close to, physically, in an age, or was there more to it than that? Yes, surely, there was. Because she knew instinctively he was attracted to her, certainly sympathetic, so that perhaps, perhaps, she stood a fair chance of "using" him. But that was for later. Now she was facing one formidable and high-handed woman who already knew too much about her, who — it dawned on her — would stop at nothing to ensure the continuation of her own committed well-being and deservedly impressive missionary work at Mtina, so she must not, must not, permit her true feelings and near-certain intentions to show. Had she already done so? No, please God. *Please*, God, give her the strength to fight this through, successfully. Prove, as she *must*, that *she* could be as formidable as anyone else, when she set her mind to it.

"You know I want you to stay on here, as part of our, on the whole, effective team, for the foreseeable future," Mother Livia said. "Provided, that is, you have learned your lesson. Have you?"

"Yes, Mother-Sister, yes, I have," she said earnestly. And immediately, playing the penitent, "I was a fool, I forgot my vows, but now, with your help — for which I'm eternally grateful — my convictions and surety of purpose have returned, and I will never again allow —"

"Because we can always get you transferred to another of our mission-stations, if you wish," Mother Livia interrupted. "It would take time, but it can be done. Or, alternatively," she went on, "if you were to decide, or have already decided, that our missionary work is not the sort of life you wish to go on leading, and your vocation has deserted you, we can start the process of releasing you from your vows and repatriating you to the UK. I can assure you, from past experience in such cases, which have indeed, if rarely, occurred in the past, that our governing council is by no means lacking in understanding —"

"*Please*! Don't go on," Jeanne said, raising her hand. "It's not necessary, I give you my word. I'm not going *anywhere* else, unless . . . unless you send me away." The lie — at least as far as driving ambition was concerned — tripped off her tongue; for a fraction of a second it shocked her, but then she thought, no, it didn't, because there was too much at stake here, vitally affecting herself and her future, for her to give even the slightest intimation of indecision now.

"All right then, I'm very glad," Mother Livia said, rising to her feet, permitting herself a brief but undoubtedly warm and friendly smile in parting. Bending down she picked up the tray, before going on, "I'll leave you the lamp." And with a gesture to Jeanne's prie-dieu, "I hope you will pray tonight, with all your heart, for Our Lord's help and guidance to keep you adamant in your faith, then get a good night's rest. In the morning I'll have a look at your back again and, if all's still well, you may resume your duties, as before."

"Thank you, Mother-Sister, I'm deeply in your debt, for everything you've done," Jeanne said. Rising to her feet also, she accompanied her superior to the door and opened it for her. Mother Livia said goodnight and then went out into the encroaching dark. Holding the door wide open, so her superior couldn't lock it again, Jeanne made certain she was on her way towards the well-lit refectory, before closing the door once more upon her departure. At once she began to shiver uncontrollably in reaction, to all that had transpired in the last half-hour. Then, still standing, biting her lip, she buried her face in her hands, sobbing once — in relief.

She was beginning to hate them now, she realized: *that* had been growing within her as well, little by little, since the morning of the day before, and had given her the will to stand and fight. Not as individuals, but as the personification and imperfect instruments of a power over her before which she had bent the knee for half a decade. Years which they had stolen from her because of her *own* weakness and stupidity, but she wasn't either weak or stupid any longer. Not so stupid as to blame God himself — Jesus, the Saviour — she still believed in Him, with all her heart. That hadn't altered. No, those she blamed were the ones who, down the centuries until today, had cravenly, or selfishly, chosen to misinterpret the Master's plan, backed away, and gone into hiding. Them. The night before last, in the hope and expectation of purging herself of sin, she had pleaded her need then submitted her cringing body to the lash in penitance and hope. For hours afterwards, until the morning, as slowly she'd recovered, she'd supposed herself cleansed. She'd been euphoric, positive, her faith restored, she believed, until she'd seen that young man again just prior to his departure. Then, her doubts had suddenly resurfaced. *Then* her mind and body had begun, directly contrary to her wishes at the time, to rebel once more. At first, by way of denial and because of the struggle going on inside her, she had come close to passing out in Mother Livia's office which had caused the Mother-Sister to insist she return to her cell to get more rest and sleep. She had accompanied her, helped her partially undress, and made sure she had all she required and was reasonably comfortable, before locking her in. And there she had fought her battles, convincing herself first one way then the other until, very gradually and as her mind cleared, the only way forward became inescapable and she began — at first tentatively, but with occasional recourse to the Saviour, in fear and explanation — to scheme.

To leave her post at Mtina, be absolved of her vows, through the tried and tested channels laid down by her Order, and as outlined by Mother Livia just now, would take too long, anything up to six months. And *now* was the time to have done, get out, before anyone had a chance to seek to persuade her to change her mind as they were bound to do. From the moment she announced her decision to leave, they would be after her and her life turned into a living hell. While it lasted, that was sure to mean sadness, bewilderment, ostracism; her fellow nuns might not mean to be dismissive, unhelpful, or even downright rude, but wouldn't be able to help themselves. She was cutting herself loose from all they believed in and held sacred. Then, in the first instance, the man whose job it would be to speak with her, advise her, attempt to revitalize her faith and hear her confession would be a man whom none of them at Mtina had a great deal of time for. Father Simon. He might be their spiritual pastor, and as such to be treated with due deference, but his opinions and involvement in their affairs had never had more than minimal impact. And after him, and in time, she'd be packed off to Lindi, where she'd be in the hands and at the mercy of strangers, hard-faced men and harder women. No, thank you; the thought was an anathema to her and such an eventuality to be avoided at almost any price, because an alternative beckoned — it surely did — and it was far too compelling for her to resist.

Around nine at night, after supper in the refectory was over, La'ali came to see her — as she'd done the night before with Mother Livia's permission, no doubt. Jeanne had been counting on the girl's arrival and by this time had her plans worked out in some detail. Over many months La'ali had become her friend; they were close — essentially two of a kind beyond the differences of age, race and status — and she was confident she had but to ask for the young African girl to do everything she could to help. Apart from that and because La'ali had confided in her, Jeanne knew of the girl's relationship with Joseph Ulaya, the government mechanic, that she slept with him whenever opportunity offered but, for many reasons, was terrified their liaison would become common knowledge and would do just about anything to prevent that happening. Another reason for Jeanne to be practically certain —

As soon as La'ali let herself in they embraced, but, before they sat down together to talk a while, Jeanne took from her the empty enamel bucket, with lid, the girl had brought with her and substituted it for the one in the commode provided for her use in the corner of her cell; took that outside the door and left it there. When she returned, La'ali was already seated at table, smiling her lovely toothy African grin and watching her with shining eyes. "You look so much better this evening, Sister," she said. "I'm so glad. You look yourself again." No one had told *her* why her friend had been taken ill two nights before, and Jeanne had no intention of voluntarily enlightening her.

She said, "Oh yes, I'm fine again today, thank you" — not the whole truth but there were other points at issue, far more important than that. How to begin because, even if this were La'ali, there was still care needed if she were to achieve all she had in mind. She had decided in the last half-hour to make her break for freedom *straightaway*. Why wait longer? So she dropped her eyes, erased the smile from her face, and said softly and seriously, "What I'm going to tell you now you tell *no one* else, La'ali. I have to have your promise on that, as God is your witness."

Startled, the African girl sat up. "What?" she murmured. "I don't understand. What is it?"

"Your promise first," Jeanne said, looking up and staring her in the eyes. "Do I have it, or not?"

"Yes, of course," La'ali said, and emotionally, "I love you, you're my best friend, you're different from the others, and —"

"All right," Jeanne interrupted her but then paused, studying the girl facing her who had risen anxiously to her feet and stood waiting. She was wearing a black blouse — her slender waist bare — a black skirt, both of which, being an excellent seamstress, she had made herself, and had a long red, black and yellow *kanga*, with the words *Duna ni Maarifa*, the World is Knowledge, imprinted on it in a couple of places, over her shoulders and round her back. They were the same height, she and the girl, Jeanne thought, yes, and their figures were nearly identical: they were both broad-shouldered, full-breasted and comparatively narrow-hipped. What one could wear, the other could also, almost certainly.

"I'm leaving here, La'ali," she said without further preamble. "I don't any longer wish to be a nun" — and, at the thunderstruck look on the girl's face, raised a warning finger to her lips. "I want to leave here before first light tomorrow morning and I want you to help me. To meet me just this side of the place where the women of your village do their washing. There, on the river-bank, as soon as daylight comes. Will you do that for me? Please?"

Slowly, her hand on the chairback, the African girl sank down into her seat again, her mouth slightly agape, her eyes blinking rapidly. All she said was, "But — but, where will you go?"

"Never mind. It's better you don't know." Then, forcefully, "Well, will you meet me? Will you do that?"

"*Why*? What do you want me to do?"

"Bring me clothes. Some of yours. Then, after I've changed into them, you must hide my habit — bury it, whatever you like — so that no one will ever find it again. After that you must forget me, get on home, and then come in to the mission as usual, as if nothing had happened."

"I cannot forget you. How can I do that?" All at once the young girl's face screwed up, and there were tears in her eyes, beginning to trickle down her cheeks. Softly she wailed, "I don't want to *do* this. I don't want you to go. Please tell me you're joking."

"I'm not joking," Jeanne said. Hastily she got to her feet, went round the table, bent and draped her arm across the girl's shoulders. When the girl looked up at her in anguish, she said, "You'll do this for me because — I swear to you before God — by doing it you'll be saving my life."

* * *

Two mornings later, around nine, after exhorting all and sundry to pull their fingers out in relation to marauding elephant and other matters (the word *dawa* not having been mentioned), John Benning left Sinyanga. At Mendi the day before things had gone well; the errant herd had been driven off westward so there was nothing further to keep him in the area. Reaching Langoro around half-eleven, he didn't go near the office but, without saying when he might return, dropped Salim at home along with most of his kit; then Nussoula at the billet he shared with two of his wives on the outskirts of town, telling the big Messenger to take the rest of the day off as he had earned it. Then he set out at once along the main road towards the turn-off to Mtina.

It was a day in high summer, very hot, the *jangwa* through which he passed parched, treeless and empty, and little sign of life in the few settlements by the roadside, as if everyone were indoors. Very sensible. One of the most barren stretches of terrain in the whole of Langoro District this, and successive DCs had done their level best to get such inhabitants as there were to move out to areas which were better watered, healthier, and where there was ample room for them, but thus far with no effect at all. They had always lived there, the people said, and didn't intend to go anywhere else, so, short of burning their hovels to the ground and moving them out by force, there wasn't any more to be done. No one was thinking of resorting to *that* particular solution, however, which had been tried elsewhere, in other districts with a similar problem, leading to much ill-feeling, and, in the long run, the people had either died out anyway or moved of their own accord. So, it was best forgotten.

Why was he going to Mtina? He'd changed his mind a second, or third time and almost not gone. It simply wasn't his business any more, he knew that — not until, at least, someone called him in again, as a corroborative witness or whatever — but still. To hell with it, he wanted to know what was happening; he wanted to see that girl again and talk to her, if he could, while knowing perfectly well his chances of doing so in private were probably almost nil. But he wanted to be sure she was all right — that, if nothing else — and to show her, by turning up again, that if she needed it, as he suspected she might, there *was* someone out there who actually cared. Barely justifiable curiosity on his part, coupled with a growing unease, it was also unwise, he was fairly certain, but never mind. Any one of at least four scenarios was liable to confront him on his arrival at the mission, given that *she* had been the one encouraging her Mother-Sister to lay into her and make her atone. Either it would be business as usual: she was recovered, forgiven, and life went on as before. Or David Morgan had spoken with the Father, and he'd been horrified; had long since arrived there, in which case the place might already be closed down, Mother Livia suspended, and the matter held in abeyance pending a full and open enquiry. Or, after talking it over, David Morgan and Father Simon might have come to the conclusion that in the interests of the mission's continuing with its good work, this incident should best be treated as an internal matter, a one-off, a singular if wholly unacceptable aberration: that Mother Livia should, therefore, merely be severely reprimanded and warned as to her future conduct, but on the quiet and, as soon as possible, the girl transferred elsewhere. Or, and at the back of John Benning's mind, this was a possibility he feared more than any other: that such had been the ferocity and severity of the girl's chastisement that without benefit of a qualified doctor's care and the right medication, her wounds were festering and, unless something were done quickly, she was likely to sicken and die. Except that no one — not even Mother Livia — would be so rabidly callous as to allow *that* to happen, would they? Ah hell, pure conjecture, all of it, and some of it way over the top, he chided himself, as he drove on, making all the speed he could. The permutations were surely endless and he'd find out what, if anything, had been going on at Mtina when he got there, and deal with, or adjust to, whatever circumstances faced him at the time. That he felt himself personally involved, to the point of rashness, perhaps, in this extraordinary sequence of events, he admitted unequivocally to himself, but — so all right, then — this bizarre situation had come up and he was ready to take on whatever further part in it fate might hand him to play. That girl out there, she'd "got through" to him — seemed to be "calling" him — and, at the very least, he wanted news of her again.

He arrived at the mission in the early afternoon to find the place deserted. No one about, no classes going on, not a soul there — except La'ali. He'd drawn up at the open gate, got out and banged on it hard with his knuckles, singing out "*Hodi*!" No one answered and, after a few moments, looking about him in surprise and already with a nagging suspicion that something must seriously be wrong, he went in; walked in the direction of classrooms, refectory and church. Halfway he met the African girl hurrying to meet him and came to an immediate halt, seeing her face which was ravaged by heart-rending emotion, sadness, and streaked with recently shed tears.

"What is it? What's *happened*?" he demanded.

But she wouldn't look at him. As if her legs would no longer support her, she folded at the knees, huddled on the ground at his feet and, before looking up at him, drew a corner of her *kanga* across the lower part of her face. Somewhat indistinctly and miserably, she said, "Sister Carmela, bwana — she *gone*!"

"What?" he asked, bending down to her. "Gone? Carmela? What're you telling me? Carmela's gone, is that it? Gone where?"

"Don't know, bwana," La'ali said, shaking her head and looking down again. "All I know, yesterday morning, she not in her room, and when they look for her, she not here." Her normally cultured Swahili seemed for the moment to have deserted her.

"And the others?" he persisted. "Where are *they*? Where have they got to?"

"Gone to villages, bwana — same as yesterday — speak with people, headmen. Ask them to search for

Carmela, bring her back. Father Simon, he arrive yesterday morning ten o'clock — he go out with them."

He straightened up. In a second, La'ali got to her feet also, to stand beside him. Eventually he said, "Why did she go, La'ali, did she say anything to you?" And, turning his head, "She's all right again, is she? She's not ill, or something?"

"No, she much better. Evening before, when I see her, she OK."

"Good — good." For the time being, he hadn't the slightest idea what, if anything, he should do, he realized, only that it didn't appear to serve any purpose for him to hang about here. No indeed, far better he got back to Langoro and report this amazing twist in events to his boss, who almost certainly knew nothing, or perhaps had been deliberately kept in the dark, about it thus far. Of course, yes —

But La'ali said, "You come with me, Bwana John, I make you nice cup of tea, in the refectory. You like that?"

"All right, thank you," he said, but then, on impulse, as she turned and began to move away, "Can I see her room, La'ali? Carmela's? Is that permissible? Is it open?"

"No, but I got the key," she said. "I show you, if you like. Come, you follow me."

So he did, wondering, as they made their way past the silent classrooms, and the church, to the line of adjoining mud and wattle cells a few yards in from the northern wall, why it was suddenly important for him to see her quarters. To learn a little more about her? To understand a little better what had induced her to call down brutal punishment on herself and, now, to run away? Yes, both of those, no doubt, but more, to be able to empathize with her, even take whichever side *she* favoured when and if the contradictions in her nature were revealed as attributable to human frailty, as he suspected, and were thus, in his eyes, forgivable. That was what true love was about, it occurred to him, between man and woman. It was a thought which had never struck him before, but, if so, it didn't apply in this case, and never would. How could it?

La'ali produced a bunch of keys, selected one and unfastened the padlock on Sister Carmela's cell door, pushed it wide, so he could enter. At first, in the poor light provided through the single barred window at the back and the doorway behind him, he could see little, but then slowly his eyes became accustomed. And, stiffening, only his eyes moving as he looked around, he hated what he saw: the austerity, the claustrophobic and empty feel of the room, the sparse and ill-made furnishings, the narrow bed; finally the prie-dieu — the Cross above it on the wall — which seemed to him to add an element of tragedy to an ambience already devoid of human warmth and self-respect. No trace of her lingered on there — except one, and this to him, as he became aware of it, only compounded the pity and sympathy for her which seized upon him without warning. The cell retained her scent, like a half-forgotten presence in the air: that of a woman and her bodily functions, her sweat; that of the salves in use upon her person prior to her escape; that of a particular woman, unique, and subtly different from the scent of any other. Encountering her in that way, in the half-dark of that unfriendly little room, was all at once nearly intolerable to him — that *she* had been subject to such indignity and humiliation — and he stepped back, turned, and rejoined La'ali outside.

"All right, yes, thank you, La'ali," he said. "A cup of tea, a cool drink, something like that. I'd be grateful." He thought that, after all, he might as well wait on here at the mission for a while before getting back to Langoro. Maybe one or all of the Sisters would return shortly; maybe they'd found her and she'd be with them.

"Why did you go out there again?" David Morgan asked. Benning had found him in the Native Treasury across the road from the District Office, going over the accounts with the clerk. They sat either side of the broad roughly made table which, with its upright chairs, lockable cupboard and massive safe beside it, were the only items of furniture which the big square red-brick room contained. David had the books spread out on the table before him, but the clerk who'd been working on them with him was now nowhere to be seen. By this time it was 4.30 in the afternoon.

"Forgot some washing they were kind enough to say they'd do for me the evening I had my accident with the car. I thought I'd go out and get it," he said. Not the truth, of course, but not something anyone was likely to check up on. "Just as well I did, I suppose."

"She's gone, you say, done a bunk?" David sat back, smoking, a frown on his face. "I wonder where she thinks she'll get to?" And he added, "Poor girl."

"No one had returned by the time I thought I'd better get back and report in," Benning said. "But, with the villagers' help, they're bound to find her, I think, sooner or later. The Father was there and had gone out with them."

"Yes, he left here yesterday morning."

"You talked things over with him?"

"Yes, I did." David nodded. "We agreed that the best thing to do before deciding what action to take, was for him to get the girl back here and have her examined by Dr Silvarosa. Had I not been in court all morning today, very probably I'd have gone out there already to see what was holding things up."

"The Father didn't raise any objections?" Benning asked. "To the girl being examined by an outside medic, a man?"

"He had no choice," David said shortly. "It was either that, or I'd be on the wire to Lindi, the PC, straightaway, after which they'd be in serious shit." He paused, and shook his head. "I thought — after all you'd told me — we should at least talk to the girl in question, and listen to what she had to say, before going any further. Maybe there were," he shrugged, "extenuating circumstances."

"Could be," Benning said. And he added quietly, a little surprised, "That was good of you."

David Morgan made a face, sitting forward again. "If there's any reason, in this matter, for us to hold back, then I believe we ought to consider it, at least. When we're in possession of all the facts, the girl's been examined and her testimony recorded, *then*, if this is really as nasty as it appears, we have no recourse but to throw the book at them. I confess I hope it doesn't come to that, but" — he gestured — "if it does, it does. They cannot be allowed to get away with it."

"I agree," Benning said. Knowing it didn't matter a lot what he thought in this case, but ready and willing to back his superior officer in whatever way he might be called upon to do so. Looking up, he went on, "So what do you want me to do now? Shall I get out there again and wait for Father Simon and the Sisters to return? Maybe they've already done so and, if they have and Sister Carmela's with them, shall I get the Father to bring her in immediately?"

For a few seconds David thought it over, before saying, "No — you hold the fort here, I'll go out there myself." He stood up. "Why don't you drop round to the house about nine this evening? I should have returned by then and I'll let you know how I've got on. Father Simon and that young nun could even be with me, staying at my place overnight." Again he shrugged. "If I'm not back, I'll probably be spending the night at the mission, going out to talk to the local *jumbes* in the morning, and so on."

"Right," Benning said, and also rose to his feet, waiting while David closed up and tidied together the ledgers and files on the table before him. Then, when the DC was finished, he ventured, "You know, I don't say the young nun — Carmela, they call her — I don't think she's blameless in this, almost certainly she isn't. But Mother Livia, she's the one, isn't she?" Frowning he shook his head. "She has to be some kind of psychopath, does she not?"

"Looks like it," David Morgan said. And, as he rounded the table, heading for the door, he murmured, "Africa does things to people. They change." He went out, into the airless heat of late afternoon in the shadow of casuarinas without turning his head, but Benning was fairly certain, at that moment, he was thinking of his wife. The same could probably be said for Carmela as well, he thought, yes, she had been out here in the bush long enough, and Mother Livia far too long! But then, given that explanation for all that had happened to date might indeed have contributory relevance, might it not also apply, to some degree, to himself?

CHAPTER SEVEN

He woke at first light, when Salim brought in his early morning tea. Noticed sleepily that when he put down his mug and saucer on the bedside table, Salim hesitated a moment, as though he thought to say something, but then didn't; drew back the curtains a little before going silently away. While, propped on one elbow, he drank his tea, he remembered the events of the previous day, ending in his going round by torchlight to David's house close on nine to find the DC not yet returned. Which meant, almost certainly, that out at Mtina, Carmela had not so far been traced and David had stayed out there to add his considerable weight to whatever extension of the search for her was planned for the morning.

It occurred to him then that to have any hope of getting clean away — as he guessed she might have wished to do — the girl must have had help at least to start with. This made him think of La'ali, who hadn't been her normal self when he'd last seen her at the mission yesterday afternoon. La'ali, yes, the possibility was surely there, because the young African girl and Carmela had reputedly been friends, and maybe La'ali had actually been grieving for her — perhaps even feeling guilty over the part she'd recently played and hadn't been finding it easy to come to terms with it. Another dreadful, but distinct possibility was that Carmela was in fact dead; they couldn't find her for *that* reason: that during the night a wild animal had got her, and La'ali, perhaps escaping with her, knew of it but wasn't letting on.

Oh hell, he thought, as he got himself out of bed, having heard Kaisi bring in his shaving water to the bathroom next door, my imagination's all over the shop, just have a shave, breakfast, then get in to work: "hold the fort" as David had put it. Because there'd be a stack of things to catch up on after his days of leave and out on safari, until such time as his superior, with or without Carmela and Father Simon in tow, returns from Mtina, and what's gone on out there and what's in prospect, is revealed. In fact, leave it be and try to get on with your job.

Naked, he padded barefoot into the bathroom, had a quick shave, nicking himself under the left ear in the process, to his annoyance — it required dabbing with cotton wool — before going back into the bedroom to dress. A complete change of clothes from the day before including, on impulse, his best shirt: a cool sea-island cotton from Harrods, purchased at Elizabeth's instigation, a day or two before his departure from Britain, when they had gone on a last-minute shopping expedition together. It had a button-down collar and broad beige stripes, and he usually kept it for special occasions but, well, he felt like indulging today. He wore it loose over beautifully pressed khaki shorts;

completed his outfit with white stockings, held in place by narrow garters, and chukka-boots. After he'd laced them up, he sat on his bed thinking for a few moments that, extraordinarily enough, this was the first time in a couple of days he'd given even a passing thought to his girl back home. There'd been far too much going on and he'd been too ruddy tired, perhaps. Nevertheless it felt to him like something of a betrayal that he'd forgotten her for so long and, briefly, he didn't like himself for it and asked her forgiveness. But he consoled himself a little with the thought that tomorrow was Friday, mail day — provided the bus got through OK from Lindi — and, with any luck, there'd be at least one letter from her, after which they'd be reunited again for a while as far as they ever could be in their present situation, before the day arrived for her to become his bride. Oh please, he begged, let the weeks pass quickly until then, please God, don't let me lose her, make her have second thoughts, or meet someone else. He'd write her a long newsy and intimate letter tonight, he vowed, to send on the bus on the morrow. He'd make the time to do it even, if necessary, into the small hours; they were the best time for it, in fact, just he and she together in the night. He could love her in his mind and bare his soul.

Dressed as the young DO on station, very much in the public eye and ready to deal authoritatively with any *shauri* which might arise, he went in to breakfast. At the end of the long room, by sideboard and fridge, the dining table was set for one, a clean white napkin, neatly folded, on his side-plate. He sat himself down, reaching out for the glass of fresh orange juice with which he liked to start things off.

Very shortly, Salim, in a belted white *kansu* and sandals, appeared from the kitchen bearing a tray laden with a plate of fried eggs on lightly toasted bread from the one small Indian bakery in town, plus (tinned) bacon, a well-stocked toast rack, a tall jug of milky coffee made with beans imported from Kenya, and a bowl of cane sugar. These, with a murmured greeting, he disposed on the table before stepping back. But he didn't depart and, tray in hand, continued to stand at his employer's shoulder. When Benning looked up at him interrogatively, he said quietly, "*Amefika bibi*, bwana. *Anakaa nje*."

"Woman? What woman?" Benning asked, eyebrows raised. "What does she want?"

"*Sijui*, bwana," Salim said uncomfortably. "She didn't say."

"OK, I'll see her as soon as I've finished breakfast," Benning said, turning away to get on with it.

"She asks," Salim said, "for you please to come quickly." And he added, "Maybe she's sick or something, I think."

"All right," Benning said after a moment, putting down his knife and fork. Easing back his chair, he got resignedly to his feet. "Where is she then, *baba*?"

"Out the back, bwana, under the big tree. She's been there waiting since before dawn, Kaisi says."

Benning nodded, frowning a little; it was unusual, to say the least, for anyone to come looking for him at home: it wasn't encouraged. So he went through and out the back door, but halted on the *stoep*, looking about him curiously. Straight ahead of him were the kitchen quarters — breeze-block walls, roof of corrugated iron, a plume of smoke rising into the still clear air from the chimney above it. To the left of that and beyond, the single giant casuarina, a towering spire of verdant hanging greenery, stood out against the pearly blue of African sky. At its foot, not far from the massive trunk, in the barren area of dust-brown murram surrounding it, huddled the woman, dressed all in black, her face hidden by the shroud of her *abeya*. Beside her, in the dust, was what looked like an ordinary school satchel.

He went down the step and towards her, knowing there was something strange about this because Salim had chosen not to accompany him and had gone back to stand in the kitchen doorway. Suddenly he guessed who this might be — *must* be, he suspected — and was so disconcerted by her arrival his mind refused to accept it straight away. She sat slumped over her knees, her face and hands hidden, her legs folded under her. She wore, what he could see of them under her *abeya*, a black long-sleeved blouse buttoned to the neck, a long black skirt which covered her to the soles of her boots. He stood over her and, in a moment, she lifted her head, drew her *abeya* away from her face with one pale hand, and looked up at him. She looked exhausted, desperately weary and in pain, yet, seeing him, essayed a tentative smile, indescribably moving, in greeting. As if to say, I did it, I got here; now it's up to you. Please forgive me for troubling you, but I know you will help me, if you can.

He extended his hands to her. She reached up and took them, held on to them strongly, and he raised her gently to her feet. She gritted her teeth, moaned once, but then straightened her back, facing him. Her face — one he'd never forget — was streaked with dirt, shiny with old sweat, her dark eyes puffy and dazed from lack of sleep. He found his voice and said softly, "Come inside now. Please, come inside and rest."

"Thank you, yes, I'd like to," she murmured.

Releasing one of her hands, he turned and drew her towards the back door. But she was very lame, her feet badly blistered no doubt, and she staggered a little, biting her lip, so, without thinking he offered her his other hand again to hold on to — which she did — while encircling her lower back and hips with his arm to support her and help her get along. From outside the kitchen door Salim and Kaisi were both watching them and, somewhat tersely, Benning called out to his houseboy to come over and assist. But Carmela, perhaps embarrassed, perhaps ashamed — in any case determined to make her own way unaided — gestured negatively and shook her head, so Salim, who had started forward, didn't approach any nearer. At the same time she disengaged herself from Benning's arm round her hips, retaining only her grip on his hand for a few seconds longer, before leaving go of that as well.

Accommodating his pace to hers, he stayed at her side, anxious she might fall any time and ready to steady her again. But she showed no sign of falling and, as soon as they reached the *stoep*, he stood back to allow her to mount first. Thanking him with a glance, she did so, and crossed it — her hand stretching out to grab on to the doorframe for a second or two — then went inside. He followed. Standing within the doorway she was looking round, her eyes blinking and, he realized at once, overcome by pity and dismay, almost out on her feet.

"Please," he invited quickly, concerned, "why don't you sit down." Noticing her eyes come to rest on his barely started breakfast on the table, he asked, "Are you hungry?"

She nodded without speaking, lowering her eyes, and he went and drew his chair further out from the table and held it for her. She came and subsided into it, but took care not to lean back, reminding him that it was only four nights ago she had been brutally whipped to the point of losing consciousness. Shakily she raised her hands, lifted her *abeya* away from her face and dark cropped hair; arranged it to lie across her shoulders and down her front before, with an uncertain smile, she turned to look up at him.

"But this is *your* breakfast, isn't it?" she said, glancing down at it again.

"Doesn't matter," he said. "Go ahead and tuck in — have some coffee. I'll get my boy to rustle up some more." And with that, he turned on his heel, strode out the back door again, and came to a halt.

Across the *stoep*, Carmela's satchel in his hand, Salim was waiting for him, Kaisi at his side. Both looked stunned, uncomprehending — much as he did himself, he supposed — but it was up to him what came next, and he tried to sort out the confusion in his mind. First things first: these two, both devoted retainers on whom he'd come to rely, were the only ones so far — he hoped, but that was as yet unproven — who knew of the girl's arrival at his house. So, until such time as it proved otherwise and she'd had the chance to rest and recover, and he the opportunity to talk to her, the news of her presence here must not be allowed to get about. That such news went unreported — by himself, or anyone else — for a matter of a few hours or even longer, shouldn't make a great deal of difference, one way or the other, later on. It was 'lay-down-the-law' time, therefore, particularly to the boy Kaisi who, being little more than a child, had been known to be a blabbermouth in the past.

But he spoke to Salim directly who, if told, and told to keep Kaisi in order, would do it, responding to John's trust in him, at least until such time as his employer relieved him of his burden of silence. He said, "*Babawe*, this woman has arrived here from Mtina, where she lives and works, as you may know, and it is not clear to me yet why she's come. I will question her as soon as I can, but she is sick and very weary after travelling so far on foot and must be allowed time to regain her strength. It may be too that I will need to get the doctor to see her before anything else. You understand?"

"Yes, bwana," Salim said.

"So, until such time as these matters are sorted out, you and Kaisi" — he turned and stared at the boy intently — "you will say nothing at all, concerning the woman's arrival here; *nothing*, to anyone. Is that clear? Not a word. This could be a matter of considerable importance to many others. I just don't know for the moment, so we'll have to wait and see."

Both Salim and the boy nodded, the man slowly and thoughtfully, the boy several times, his eyes popping, before Salim asked, "The woman will stay here, bwana. In your house?"

"Yes," Benning said. "For the time being. I will be going in to the office shortly but before I do I'll tell her to stay inside until I get back. If, by any chance, she tries to leave before I return, or does so, you, Kaisi, will run to the office, find me and let me know." He smiled at the boy. "All right?"

"Yes, bwana *mkubwa*," Kaisi said shyly.

"What if others know already that she is here?" Salim asked. "If they come, what shall we say to them?"

Benning thought it over carefully for a second or two, looking aside and frowning. Then he said, "Before I return the only person who gets in to see her, and talk to her, if he comes, is the DC. Only him, no one else, not even someone from her mission, whoever it might be. If they come you tell them, politely, no, sorry, but those are your orders. Got that?"

"As you say, bwana," Salim said.

Taking Carmela's satchel (containing what? — a torch, an empty bottle of water, maybe a few crumbs of food?) from Salim, Benning turned to look in through the open doorway into his dining-cum-sitting-room. Across the room, to his left, her hands hidden, Carmela remained at the table, eyes down on his empty plate before her, the toast-rack empty also. As he watched, she lifted a hand and took up his coffee mug, raised it to her lips and drank — and so noticed him.

He nodded to her, but immediately turned again, saying to Salim over his shoulder, "She's had my breakfast, *baba*, so you better cook up some more, please, and fix another jug of coffee. OK?"

"Five minutes," Salim said impassively, and he and Kaisi left.

Benning entered the room, pulled up another upright chair and sat down, facing her, the satchel on the tabletop beside him. To bridge the silence and give his hands something to do, he took out a packet of cigarettes and began lighting up. She said contritely, "I'm so sorry, I've eaten everything. I was so hungry."

"You're welcome," he said. "More's on the way. You feel a little better?"

"Oh yes, thank you," she said. "But now" — she dropped her eyes, but quickly lifted them once more — "now I'd like to use your bathroom, if I may?"

"Of course," he said, getting to his feet again. "I'll show you." And, as she too stood up and he indicated the doorway into his bedroom, he added, "After that, when you're ready, Carmela, you and I have to talk."

She looked at him searchingly, so that, *not* for the first time, he was struck by the realization that, never mind all she'd been through, he found her seriously attractive both facially and in her slender provocative figure — among other things her bare midriff drew his eye. She invoked his allegiance as a man, protectively and for far more primitive reasons. Quietly she said, "I'm not Carmela any more. I want you to know that. That's why I'm here. Please, try to remember — my name's Jeanne Rawson, and I'd like you to call me Jeanne."

"I will," he said and, passing her as she stood waiting, pointed out to her, through his bedroom, the bathroom door on the other side. "Through there," he said. "And if you don't find everything you need, just give a shout. I'll be out here."

"Thank you, you're very kind," she said. But then, looking up at him and her dark eyes unequivocal in their appeal, added quietly, "Be patient with me, John, please, if you can. Don't be cross with me for coming here. I knew of no one else, not another soul, to whom I could turn, and you seemed —" But she didn't say any more; left him and continued on her limping way. He watched her retreating back until she disappeared into the bathroom, closing the door behind her. Cross? He didn't feel *cross*, no, not in the slightest. More like glad, favoured, he couldn't deny it.

He returned to the dining-table and sat down, thinking; he relit his cigarette, then lowered his head and rubbed his forehead with his free hand. To betray her presence here or not, that was the dilemma which confronted him. He knew what he *ought* to do, of course, but for the moment felt entirely disinclined to do it. Not, at least, until he'd heard what she had to say and listened to whatever plans she'd had which had brought her to his door. It had been one hell of a long way to come, on foot and mostly at night, as appeared to be what she'd done. It had surely taken some doing, and fortune had been extraordinarily kind to her. Among other things it had taken courage, and he could not but respect that.

Salim brought him fresh helpings of eggs, bacon and fried bread, more toast and another jug of coffee. After serving him he rounded the table to take up Jeanne's empty mug and used plates on his tray, then stood waiting.

"That's it then, *baba*, thank you," Benning said, picking up the knife and fork with which Salim had also equipped him, and beginning to eat. "I'll call you when I've finished."

"*Hasua*, bwana," Salim said, and departed once more.

Nothing further happened for a while: minutes passed as he ate what had been set before him. Then he unfastened the straps and took a look inside the girl's satchel still at his elbow and found it empty, so set it down on the floor. Then he thought he heard a noise from beyond the closed bathroom door and sat suddenly quite still, waiting for the sound, or sounds, to be repeated. They were, loud enough for him to identify them as somewhere between a cry and a groan and, instantly, he was out of his chair, across the room and into his bedroom. He came to a halt, head lowered, outside the bathroom door, listening. Her cry, a distressed choking sound — a plea for mercy? — came again, and he wrenched at the doorhandle, forcing the unlocked door open against the weight of her body, slumped against it. When he got himself through the narrow opening, he found her sprawled on the tiled floor, on her side, her hands clutching at her face.

He crouched beside her, whispering, "What is it? What can I do? Tell me."

"My back, it hurts," she said, looking up at him wild-eyed, her agony vividly revealed. "It's bleeding again. Do you have something to put on it? An antiseptic cream, something like that?"

He did, in fact, have a tube of Germolene — would that suffice? — in the cupboard in his bedroom; so he nodded, but said, "I'll go for the doctor. Carmela, I have to do that. Here," he said, trying to get an arm under her, to lift her into a sitting position, and maybe help her at least as far as his bed next door.

"*No doctor*!" she cried. "No, *please*! You have something, you say, so *you* do it!" With a moan, half-stifled, she struggled to sit up, supporting herself on one arm, until her face was nearly level with his. "Oh hell, I'm so woozy," she murmured through parted lips, her eyes closing. "I can't — I can't get at my back, to do it, you know, so you, please, you must do it for me." She gave him her hands, one at a time. He held them and, slowly rising to his feet, raised her with him. Immediately she freed herself and leaned against him, lifting her arms and grabbing on to his shoulders; only then did she open her eyes again, breathing hard, her face pressing against his chest.

He gave her a minute to recover from the effort she'd made. Inevitably, then, he caught the powerful odour of her body; not a pleasant one: a combination of old sweat, soiled clothing, unwashed woman, previous medication and, perhaps, festering wounds. Holding his breath he tried to ignore it; turned her as gently as he could; guided her unprotesting through the doorway towards his unmade bed. But she wouldn't lie down on it, not yet. She halted at the bedside and stared at him across her shoulder along the corners of her eyes.

"Please, turn your back," she said quietly. "I'm going to take off my blouse."

"All right," he said uncomfortably, and did, moving away; hearing the small sounds she made divesting herself of (La'ali's?) blouse; hearing also her laboured breathing and, at one point — as she strained to get it off — the whimper of frustration and pain which escaped her lips. Then he heard her lay herself down on the bed and stretch out, the small creaking of springs — and turned again.

She lay naked to the waist, on her front, her head down on the pillow and face averted between sinewy hands. Her back was beautiful, tapering, narrow-waisted, slim-hipped, or would have been but for the big square of lint — stained here and there with old and recent blood — which covered most of it and which was held in place by broad strips of surgical tape which at the edges had often worked loose.

Murmuring, "Jesus God!" he bent over her. Then he asked, "What do you want me to do?"

"Get it off," she said. "Never mind it's stuck in places. I'll try not to scream, but it has to come off and then you can doctor it."

She was right, of course, and he knew it, but did not relish one little bit what lay in prospect, knowing he was bound to hurt her and, possibly, inflict on her greater harm than she had suffered already.

When he hesitated, she snapped, "*Come on*! Don't be such a baby — Just *do it*!" And, glancing up at him, "*Please*!"

So, his hands and fingers trembling a little and occasionally clumsy, he set about it. Teasing up and lifting back the strips of surgical tape, one side of the pad of lint; touching her warm, softly resilient and lightly freckled skin with a feeling close to reverence, not to mention dread. Then he began peeling back the pad itself, little by little, stopping when it stuck but driving himself to go on, pulling it away as carefully as he knew how from what lay beneath. The sweat stood out on his forehead; beneath him she groaned, shuddered, buried her face in his pillow and hung on to keep herself from crying out. But she held sufficiently still until the pad came away entirely and he straightened up, closing his eyes and holding it dangling from the fingers of one hand.

"How does it look?" she demanded. "Is it bad?"

He bent forward again and examined her: the criss-cross of raised weals from the whipping she'd undergone — there were many of them — one upon the other. Thinking, in horror, some of this was *my* doing, this mess. I could have prevented a lot of it, yes, I might have, had I *acted*, out at Mtina that night when I had the chance, instead of — But gritting his teeth and looking closer, though in places her wounds were suppurating and unhealed, one or more of which he'd surely torn open again, moments ago, it reassured him a little to see they were actually not as angry or infected as he'd feared. In fact, given a bit of luck, further medication, care and plenty of rest, she could well be over the worst. He prayed so, anyway, and breathed a conditional sigh of relief, stepping back.

"Can you?" she asked, staring up at him again. "Can you do what's necessary? Have you got some stuff?"

"Yes, maybe," he said, trying to think, and suddenly feeling more than a touch faint himself. "And if I haven't," he added quietly, "I can get it." Going over to his almirah by the front window, he opened it and slid out the top drawer and ran his eye over all it contained. A tube of Germolene, cotton wool, a pack of lint, a big roll of surgical tape, scissors, among other things: his first-aid kit in case of emergency. But initially, he thought, her wounds would need cleaning up with warm water with a little Dettol in it, and those he'd get, a shallow basin as well, from his bathroom and the kitchen out back. Selecting what he would need from within the drawer first, he turned to rejoin her —

To find her sitting up on the side of his bed, her arms crossed over her breasts, smiling. He hesitated a moment, but at once went on towards her, the dressings he'd gathered together in either hand. Immediately she reached out her arms to him, thereby revealing her breasts, young, darkly nippled and of astonishing beauty, saying, "Oh you, John Benning, I *knew* you would help me if I came to you." And, at his look, "Don't tell me you've never seen the naked body of a woman before."

CHAPTER EIGHT

He was hers, she thought exultantly, after he'd left for the office half an hour later. He was a dish — a bit young, yes, but all the better, and in a while, soon, she would repay him. Eagerly and gladly; she could hardly wait! Until the time arrived for her to use him further and, if her still-tentative but exciting plans proved feasible, hang on here at his house in secret; then, with his help, get away and out of Africa.

God, but it had been wonderful, for all the passing discomfort and even fleeting pain it had caused her: the touch of a man's hands again — strong worshipping hands, in tenderness, commiseration and blatant and barely restrained lust, as he'd ministered a little clumsily to her back and blistered feet, in a silence broken only by their breathing and, once, the giggles she'd made no effort to subdue when inadvertantly, then deliberately, he'd tickled her. She hadn't wanted it to stop, that was the truth; came very close, when he was nearly done, to throwing herself at him body and soul there and then, but hesitated, suspecting, probably wisely, that the moment might not be quite right yet, for him, for her to turn over, reach up, and drag him fiercely to her; entreat him with pleading eyes, swollen mouth, urgent breasts and questing hands, as she longed to do. Then he was gently covering her over with a sheet, straightening up and standing at her side, for the time being emotionally exhausted.

On the wall in his sitting-room hung the framed photo of a beautiful girl, a young blonde, doubtless the one he was eventually going to marry back home, and of whom he'd spoken during the course of that drive — that fraught journey of re-discovery — from Masasi to Mtina. She'd noticed it while eating his breakfast and recalled it more than once in the time he'd been treating her. It exhilarated her, it brought up all the woman she was and had ever been, making her writhe internally, her pudenda to itch and dilate, leaking and demanding attention — her nipples aching in response and starting to drive her frantic — the prospect of *fighting* another woman with her body, *and* intelligence, for a man's love and sexual devotion and finally *beating* her, at least temporarily, as she would, she fully intended. And if, later, he felt he had to confess his fall from grace — call her his "bit on the side" — to that other, then more fool him. If she then broke off their engagement, cooled towards him, because of what he'd told her, even more fool her.

But suppose on his arrival at his office this morning and with the return of his superior, maybe in the company of that futile Father and virago Mother Livia, he could not contain it, or let it slip, or had already decided that as an upright young man, a highly promising DO and aspiring pillar of the Service, he *had to* report where she was — and she'd *missed her chance*, the one chance she'd ever get, to seduce him? Hell no, she thought, sitting up in his bed, massaging between her legs where she was on fire to accommodate and serve him, and gradually beginning to smile: she had *felt* the mounting passion clawing at him, the physical hunger and inclination; known that, as time passed and abandoning any thought that she was still a nun, he'd been holding himself in check only because he'd believed her to be in greater pain, more exhausted, and thus uninterested, than she was, but was truly mad for her and, having been celibate too long, such moral scruples as he might possess were on the very cusp of being blown away. To the extent, she believed, that he would say nothing — *not yet*, at any rate — giving her all the second chance she needed to bend him to her wiles and will. Of that she was intuitively, but, all at once, confidently convinced. All the same, it occurred to her then that it might be crucially important he really loved her — or thought he did — in addition to a near-overwhelming desire to indulge with her in an hour's consensual and primitive sex — and for *that* to come about she might well require a little longer. Unless he did, she suspected, she wasn't all that sure, even now, of persuading him to do her bidding unquestioningly, in the end. So time, yes, time; she only prayed she'd be permitted, or could provoke, enough.

She *was* two women, she thought. Nothing strange in that — most women were, by training, even preference, human, but animal beneath — but in a way more compelling, she could only assume, than many others of her gender. In the face of disaster, six wasted years ago, she'd seen fit, hysterically no doubt, to dispense with the emptiness, irrelevance and loneliness of her life at that time as a normal, sexually emancipated and attractive, but cruelly bereaved, young woman. Had decided she wanted no more of the anguish, terrible dreams and feelings of guilt and loss which were making her life hell on earth, and, by way of penance and some hope of deliverance had espoused a different existence of service and self-denial which, on the whole, had given her renewed confidence, comforted her, and allowed her at least the solace of a surrogate vocation. Then, just five days ago, two events had broken the mould, one following hard on the other. First, the arrival of a young, physically disturbing male with whom she'd been cooped up for several tormented and, as it was to prove, conclusive hours; second, with the objective at the time of exorcizing her own failings and his potent allure from her mind once and for all, the whipping she'd pleaded for and endured as a punishment and corrective to her errant thoughts which, as she'd realized very quickly afterwards, had had no salutary effect on her at all. She wanted desperately to rejoin the world, *that* was the basic truth of her *volte-face* of recent provenance: her whole being and underlying sensual nature were suddenly crying out for that and would brook no refusal, and the courage and determination which she'd never lacked — recklessness and tunnel-vision some would call it — had impelled her on. Go after him, for a start and, if everything went wrong, or she'd misjudged him, then to hell with it, she'd take whatever came. What lay ahead of her, in the coming hours and days, given her luck held, thrilled her, meant no alternative course of action stood a chance and, in her heart, she revelled in the risks she was taking. That was life too, and part of her, the part she welcomed with open arms, *now*.

So be it. She swung her legs over the side of his bed; stood still until a few seconds of faintness passed. Then she crossed to his almirah and chest of drawers beside it; opened doors and drawers until she found items of clothing she liked the look of: a white shirt of his to cover her loosely from shoulder to thigh, a colourful batik sarong to tie round her at the hips and fall gracefully to within an inch of the ground. Quickly she divested herself of La'ali's long dark skirt, the now-soiled undergarment beneath it. Once dressed again she went to stand before his three-quarter-length mirror on the wall to see how she looked. She looked good, and better than that, she thought, after undoing a couple of buttons on the shirt and striking a pose or two, hand on hip — a lithe, enticing young temptress and an open invitation to any man worth a cracker, as she was sure he was, to try his luck. Unremarkably perhaps, it barely crossed her mind that, after six years of total abstinence, she might have forgotten how to use her gifts, to arouse, pleasure and then hold a man, or if it did, very briefly, then such fleeting anxiety was consigned to limbo in a flash. *She knew* who she was — the six years in between had virtually ceased to exist — had, since the age of seventeen, been confident of her power. She had used it very satisfactorily on a number of occasions. That sort of sensual and aggressive magnetism: challenge, holding out the conditional promise of surrender, never left one, she believed, not until you were in your dotage anyway, if then!

Having found fresh clothes which pleased her and topped up her already revitalized self-esteem, she took them off again, and padded through into the bathroom where she would have a comprehensive wash all over, everywhere she could reach.

Had David been at his desk by the time John arrived at the office at a quarter to ten, it was more than likely he would have betrayed her, he suspected afterwards. He certainly gave it thought during the course of the morning, what he should do — whether to give her up (a distasteful, also arguably, shameful proposal) or not — which he waited for his superior officer to put in an appearance. But he didn't, and was presumably still co-ordinating the search out at Mtina which, while he got on with his work, tempted Benning towards one of two courses of action, one immediate and responsible, the other ongoing and even, conceivably, longterm. The first, to get in his car, go out to the misson, there to find the DC and tell him he could discontinue his enquiries, admitting he knew where the girl was; or, to sit tight and wait, and when the DC came back, say — nothing! Of course, to allow his superior officer *and* friend to go on wasting his time was truly reprehensible, unprofessional and dishonest, but the alternative, betrayal, outright and callous betrayal, was unquestionably worse, and with the image of that brave, badly hurt, seductive and otherwise friendless, girl in mind was not a denouement for which he was prepared to settle. No, not for a while yet, or until unforseeable circumstances forced his hand.

So, pricking up his ears on the few occasions some vehicle approached the District Office along the main road, and with the distraction among other things of a couple of minor court hearings at which he officiated during the course of the morning, he got through the hours until lunchtime. His thoughts harked back at every opportunity to that girl he had left at his house — was she still there? She must be, or Kaisi would have come to tell him of her departure, and he could not but admit to himself that to see her again, spend some time with her, talk to her, enjoy her dark femininity with his eyes — even for a limited period — was a pleasure he anticipated not only with a kind of elemental longing but also compelling interest.

So, on the stroke of 12.30, and still no sign of David nor word from Mtina, he left his office, leaving clerks and Messengers to look after the place and put their feet up during the midday break, and set off for home, saying he'd be back at two, as usual. But he didn't take his car. He walked as he often did at this time of day when he was on-station, but today in an effort to compose himself and let a little more time elapse, to get things in perspective, before facing up to a situation which, he was beginning to realize and if he allowed it to do so, might well have the makings of a personal nemesis. For that reason he didn't return to his bungalow directly, but, as a sop to his conscience and, no doubt, giving way to further moments of uncertainty and indecision, he stopped by at the DC's house *en route*; mounted the steps in the welcome shade of tamarind and casuarina, crossed the veranda and knocked on the flyscreen door.

Patti apeared in a hurry, out of the half-darkness within. Pushing open the flyscreen and holding it wide with an outflung arm against its springs, she glowered at him saying, "Oh, it's you! What d'you want?" as if she might have been expecting someone else: not her husband, surely, who was unlikely to knock on his own front door! But for once the neurotic tension which seemed to have her in a state of barely suppressed fury night and day was not so much in evidence. She wore a gorgeous housecoat of Spanish brocade buttoned to the neck which flattered her coarsening figure, and her slightly raddled features looked better cared-for and thus less combative, for the application of a little eye-shadow and lipstick. Nevertheless, she didn't like him: his youth and rugged good looks reproached her in a way too belittling to define, and she didn't bother to disguise it.

Her antipathy towards him was entirely reciprocated. She dismayed him — he hadn't a clue how to cope with her — and his sympathy for David usually made him keep his distance. However, today, having got there — as a precaution, really, in case things didn't work out — he asked politely, "The DC not back yet?" and, when she shook her head, "I'm off to have some lunch. If he returns in the next hour or so, would you be kind enough to send someone round to the bungalow? I — I may need to see him urgently, in private, as soon as he gets in."

"Why?" she snapped.

"Nothing important," he murmured, looking away. "A station matter, that's all."

"To do with that nun who's gone missing out at Mtina?"

Was she reading his mind? It confused him. "No — yes — connected with that maybe," he admitted uncomfortably, wishing now he'd had the sense to stay away from here, away from her and seeking to escape as soon as possible.

Not difficult! "All right, I'll tell him," she said; stepped back and allowed the flyscreen door to swing to and slam in his face. He turned and recrossed the veranda, fuming quietly and annoyed with himself for revealing what little he had. It was none of her damn business what he might want to see David about, no, none. Bloody woman. In fact, he found it difficult to think of her, relate to her, as a woman at all. Women weren't supposed to be like she was, not in his book.

At the foot of the steps he was about to set off again for home when he noticed someone approaching along the drive, under the casuarinas: an African, Joseph Ulaya, the station mechanic, a stocky figure in dark-blue overalls and holding a wheelbrace in one hand. Jumping to the obvious conclusion, Benning called over, "He's not back yet, Joseph, still out at Mtina."

"OK, I'll come round again later," Joesph replied and, turning on his heel, he raised his free hand in parting, before retracing his steps, walking fast. Frowning, Benning watched him go for a few moments, thinking there was perhaps something a little strange about Joseph coming to the DC's house in the middle of the day when he'd know almost certainly the DC wasn't home. Then he dismissed his curiosity and formless suspicion from his thoughts as irrelevant, having in immediate prospect a reunion with a girl who wished him to call her Jeanne Rawson, to which, in vivid recollection of her unsettling physical allure and defiant reliance on his personal assistance, he looked forward now more than ever, with a whole raft of mixed feelings maybe, but undeniable stirrings of covert and wholly unprincipled lust as well.

But when, sweating and thirsty by this time, he arrived at his house it was to find Salim awaiting him on his veranda. As he came up, his servant and trusted retainer said quietly, "*Analala sasa, bibi*" — with a glance and a gesture along the veranda in the direction of his bedroom. "The woman is asleep."

He nodded once in acknowledgment and mounted the step. Keeping his voice down, said, "Is she? That's good." After a moment's hesitation, he walked silently along the veranda on rubber soles, tried the handle on his bedroom door, found it unbolted and, making hardly any sound, opened it and went through, closing the door quietly behind him and watching her all the time as she lay sleeping there in the half-dark of drawn curtains, overcome by pity and humbling emotion.

She lay on her side, facing him, lips parted, eyes closed, one arm across her breasts and one hand beneath her chin, the lower half of her shapely body, her long elegant legs bent at the knee, clearly distinguishable under the light covering of the single sheet she'd drawn over her to her hips. Above that she was wearing a white shirt of his, he noticed — a poignant touch — the sleeves rolled to the elbow. She looked more defenceless and vulnerable than any exhausted and resting creature he had ever seen in his life before. This, *this* was woman — not the harridan who stalked the DC's domain — one who, in her young beauty and present need, demanded his unquestioning allegiance. She brought up in him all his longing to succour and cherish the opposite sex plus the injunction that because she had turned to him, he should not, under any circumstances, throw her to the wolves. And if, after a while, this led her to a desire to reward him as her lover — that was a possibility, was it not? — well, he wouldn't hesitate to accept her offering and make the most of it, for both their sakes, never mind the consequences, whatever they might be. Should it happen it would be a temptation too fundamental to back away from or resist and, in all honesty, he'd find it unthinkable, even contemptible, to pretend otherwise. Or was he beginning to assume far too much? No, almost certainly not, he believed. She'd already given him so many hints — hadn't she? — by way of testing him and drawing him inexorably to her beckoning flame, that there was no going back now to the time of innocence before her arrival. No, not any more.

Quietly he let himself out of the room, went along to his sitting-cum-dining-room where, once again, Salim awaited him. "Lunch, *baba*," he said, taking his seat.

"She will eat with you, bwana?" Salim asked.

"No, I left her still sleeping. She may want something after I've returned to the office and, if she does, give her whatever you have. This morning, did anyone come here, looking for her?"

"No, bwana, no one."

"Good," he said, and added quietly, "Let's hope it stays that way. I've not told anyone, either. Now" — he looked Salim in the eye, telling him as best he could that they were together in this and he relied on his absolute discretion — "my *chakula*, if you please. I'm hungry."

"*Dakika*, bwana," Salim said and, heading for the back door, left the room. Did he have the suggestion of a smile on his face, as he made his exit, Benning wondered? Maybe he did, and if so, it mattered not one paltry iota as long as Salim remembered not to breathe a word concerning the girl's continuing and clandestine presence here at his house and made absolutely certain Kaisi did the same; that was all he, John Benning, asked of him. That Salim might suspect his employer's motives, to derive quite genuine pleasure from the thought of his young and patently virile bwana acting the man (with a woman of his own race) — at last! — was hardly a cause for embarrassment, let alone prurient censure. In fact, very likely it would only *enhance*, Salim's liking and respect for the youthful government officer who paid his wages. With all the chances Benning had of tupping any woman hereabouts who caught his fancy, it was about time, made him more human, no doubt, in other men's eyes, and that it, or something like it (if he were reading the signs aright) hadn't happened before to Salim's certain knowledge, only went to show what an unfathomable lot these *wazungu* often were . . .

She joined him when he was well on into his main course of shepherd's pie, snake gourd and sweet potato. Though he'd been listening he hadn't heard her moving about before his bedroom door opened and she came in. She stood a moment in the doorway, blinking, as if momentarily the light hurt her eyes; then yawned hugely behind her hand and shook herself, before coming forward, an apologetic smile on her face. He pulled his chair back and stood up to welcome her, thinking, my God, but *truly* she's a looker — her expressive eyes, her passionate mouth, the easy grace with which she moves. I don't believe I've ever had the good fortune to know or even meet a girl as fascinating to me as this. I don't mind her hair, I like it that way — it's different and it suits her — and the fact she's wearing clothes of mine — that big shirt worn outside over one of my favorite sarongs; that she has no sandals or shoes to wear and so chooses to walk barefoot, doctored blisters notwithstanding — all this, in combination, leaves me lost for words. And if she is aware of my sudden shyness, that doesn't bother me either: I'll get over it soon enough, with any luck. In the meantime, he held out a chair for her and, smoothing the sarong beneath her with both hands, she slipped down into it, thanking him with a glance.

Looking up at him, she said, “I’m so sorry, I was asleep when you came in. I didn’t mean to be.” And, softly, “Is — is everything all right?”

“I’ve not let on to anyone else you’re here,” he said quietly. And, on impulse, to set her mind at rest, “Nor do I intend to.” So, it was said, and meant — his decision finally taken, for better or worse — and he knew at once that in existing circumstances, there had been no other he’d have found it even remotely possible to live with.

“I’m deeply, deeply grateful,” she murmured, and breathed a sigh of relief. Studying him, as he sat beside her and picked up his spoon and fork again to go on with his meal, she leaned forward and rested her smooth forearms on the table. “But it can’t go on indefinitely, can it?” she said. “I have to get away from here. I owe it to you to be on my way as soon as possible.” She lowered her voice. “But to achieve that, I’m going to need your help, if you — if you’ll be kind enough . . .?” She was pleading with him, unequivocally, with eyes and hands.

He sat back, watching her — in thrall to her, but over his shyness. Eventually he nodded seriously, before essaying a rueful smile. He said, “I’ll do everything I can, I promise you, just tell me what it is you have it in mind to do.” But then, seeing Salim waiting by the open back door, he added, “Only, not this minute. In a little while I have to return to the office. You have some lunch, lie low, and we’ll talk things over this afternoon

— there'll be plenty of time then. How's your back?" He signalled for Salim to come in.

"Better," she said. "Much better. Thank you again for all you did."

"I'll have another go at it later today if you think I should."

"Maybe yes, if you don't mind." She turned and lifted her head to look up at Salim who had come to a halt beside her, clean plates and cutlery in hand. Greeted him, smiling warmly, and said in fluent Swahili, "*Babawe*, you are a man of integrity and compassion, I sense that, and you realise, I'm sure, that you hold my life in your hands. Not only that but you know if it gets about I'm here, or have been here, your bwana, who has befriended me, may get into serious trouble. So I ask you, I beg you, not a word, *ever*." She held out her hand to him at shoulder height, open and palm up, inviting him to take it. After a moment, nodding slowly, he did so; held it briefly, in surprised affirmation of what could only be taken as his devotion and personal fealty to her, before she concluded soberly, "I'll not be here long. I'll be away just as soon as I can, I assure you of that, believe me."

"You're welcome here, *mama*," Salim said quietly. Leaning over her as she sat back he set plates and cutlery before her; reached out to fill her glass with water from the jug on the table. Stepped aside and salaamed then — right hand to forehead — before saying, "I make baked custard in the kitchen. It's ready when you call." And, with that, he made to depart.

From the heart, Benning said, "Thank you, Salim. We will."

And so it began, their first meal together. She had some catching up to do, and he didn't hurry her, asking her permission — readily granted — to take a break and have a smoke between courses. It was a quiet time, of familiarization and increasing wonder; for sidelong appreciation and for the call-signs of gender to have their say. Also recognition of a growing rapport between them, making it near-impossible for either of them to back away, which was leading them as if in chains towards . . .

Shortly after 3.30 a weary David Morgan returned to Langoro, and went straight to his office. After telling the Messengers to apologize to anyone waiting to speak to him and come back again in the morning, he called John in to see him. As Benning crossed the big room to his desk, the DC leaned forward and said without preamble, "She's gone — Sister Carmel. There's no trace of her, I'm afraid. I went with Mother Livia and the other Sisters to all the villages around Mtina, I drove to the main road and checked along there, but no one admits to seeing her, so she's disappeared off the face of the earth, at least for the time being."

"Could someone be hiding her?" Benning asked, standing before the desk. He had to contribute something, he felt.

"Could be," David Morgan said, and shrugged. "Seems certain she must have had help in getting away, but beyond that your guess is as good as mine."

"So, what will we do?" Benning asked, taking a seat on one of the upright chairs before the DC's desk, his face expressing interest but, he hoped, no more than professional concern. In fact, he was unquestionably tense and knew he had to be extremely careful.

"I think," David Morgan said, frowning, "before taking the steps which may be required, I'll give it another night and all tomorrow at least. She could yet turn up somewhere, or we'll get news of her. But, if we don't, then, I suppose, the most likely presumption has to be that she's dead. A leopard got her in the night, dragged her body off into the bush, and no one's found her remains so far, that's all."

"Maybe they never will," Benning said.

"It's a possibility," David conceded, rubbing his tired eyes with one hand and sitting back. "Nevertheless, I'm tempted to throw the book at that arrogant creature, Mother Livia, and order the place closed down. But in order to justify that to Lindi, we'd have to have corroborative proof of malpractice at the mission and, unless someone talks, or we find the body, we're not liable to get it." Then he added, "That visiting Father of theirs, he's no help at all, but then I didn't expect him to be."

"Mother Livia, you spoke to her? She denies everything, I suppose."

"Of course. I taxed her, in private, yesterday morning, with what you'd told me you'd seen going on in the church that night, and she laughed in my face. Then said you must be out of your mind and should be transferred elsewhere."

“So?” Benning asked, shaking his head.

“So, give it time, a bit more time,” David said. “That’s all we can do. Something may yet provide us with a lead.”

“And failing that, what then?”

“Our hands are tied. Having reported the mysterious disappearance of one of their nuns, the place will continue to function and get on with its work. What the mission authorities choose to do about said disappearance is, of course, for them to decide but I can’t see anything coming of that.”

“But, if she’s *not* dead, where might she have gone?”

“I can only think down to the coast,” David said. “Where else? She might have had a friend down there, or at Masasi — though no one at Mtina can confirm that she did — and this person, man or woman, collected her following her escape and ensured she got clean away before anyone raised the alarm. But that’s conjecture,” he said, “and surely too far-fetched by half from what little we know.”

“I agree,” Benning said.

“Anyway,” David Morgan went on, “by the time I left Mtina this afternoon, Father Simon had already taken off for Masasi to see if anyone there knew anything of her whereabouts. If not, he’ll go straight on to Lindi and start making enquiries that end. If he comes up with news of any sort, he promised me he’ll send us a wire at once. Only hope he remembers to do it.”

“OK, then,” John Benning said, his relief well hidden. “For the moment we just wait, is that right?”

“Mm, that’s it,” David said, and rose stiffly to his feet. “Now,” he said, “I’m going home to have a beer, a shower and a bite to eat, then put my feet up. I’ve had enough for one day. You stick around here and, if nothing’s changed by then, you go on home at half-five as usual and forget it till morning. If Mother Livia sends word this evening, or during the night, it’ll come to me at home, but I can’t think there’ll be any need for anyone to go out there again until tomorrow.”

“Not unless she’s injured,” Benning said quietly. “Which God forbid. Then they might need a doctor urgently.”

“Yes, there’s that,” David Morgan acknowledged, stretching and easing his shoulders. “But, if that’s the case, I’ll handle it. He’s here, is he, Dr Silvarosa?

“As far as I know,” Benning said. “He was certainly here an hour ago because I saw him walking down into town.”

“Good.” Then David paused thoughtfully a second or two longer, before going on, “It’s not *like* that, though, you know, I suspect. She’s a hundred miles away by this time, or gone to ground somewhere — *that’s* the truth of it, I think.”

“May well be,” Benning said. He hadn’t moved yet from his seat. “What little I’ve seen of her, the time she was with me coming back from Masasi, she didn’t strike me as a fool. She wouldn’t risk her life at night — as she must have done — unless she had some definite place in mind to go.”

“Unless — unless she was desperate,” David said.

That made Benning think again of Mother Livia, the plain, hard, enigmatic face of experience, faith (of a kind) and authority. Then he contrasted that face and aura in his mind with that of the young, ardent and provoking countenance, also physical and personal impact, of the girl now at his house, whose injuries he had dressed, whose exhausted, lissom and maltreated body he had cared for. She was almost certainly no saint, he'd realized, a touch regretfully, by this time, and the way she'd handled Salim at lunchtime only tended to bear that out. It had been very skilfully — perhaps a fraction *too* skilfully? — done, but, to be honest, who needed saints in this world? Maybe some did, but not him, especially, if he gave it a few seconds' thought, as far as womankind was concerned.

Moving on again towards the door, David said finally, "I'm off then. Give me a call if anything comes up."

"Will do," John said, and rose to his feet as his superior made his way out. So far, he thought, he hadn't put a foot wrong, or said anything stupid, while keeping the actual situation under wraps — thank Christ! It hadn't been easy, with David's, albeit weary, eyes upon him; and he was a little surprised their first meeting that day had passed off quite so smoothly. Next time, if there was one, would surely be less fraught. He could only pray that nothing unforeseen might occur to alter the status quo — for a night and another day, anyway.

He was reminded suddenly though of what he had said to Patti Morgan at midday, which could yet land him in big trouble and lead to the girl's current whereabouts coming to light. It surely could — cretin that he had been — but, he quickly reassured himself, it was highly unlikely it would. In her offhand way, Patti might well pass on to her husband the garbled message which he had left with her hours ago, his pathetic slip of the tongue included; but on the other hand, by this time she'd very probably forgotten it altogether, or, taking into account the parlous state of their marriage, simply not bother to mention it. Dependent on which — if she hadn't forgotten and did tell him — was David really likely to pay a lot of attention? Get back to him later to ask him exactly what he'd meant, or been referring to? It was a faint possibility, he supposed, and after the conversation which he and his DC had just concluded, he'd better be ready with some sort of plausible explanation.

Ah, to hell with it, Benning thought, following his superior officer out onto the veranda to see David on his way, all at once he'd had enough of his own spineless thinking, of trying to weigh up pros and cons and come to terms with the vagaries of chance — and it was about time he stopped! He'd never before in his entire life been a worrier, as far as he remembered: life had been too full; had mostly been plain sailing, he surmised. It hadn't been in his temperament, at the time, but it was undoubtedly a fact that, since that night at Mtina, he'd never ceased to worry for long — have doubts, and struggle with his conscience — and he didn't like it as it made him out to be the kind of man he neither saw, nor wished, himself to be. So, he warned himself, snap out of it, and do it right now, because even if he'd never faced a situation anything like this one which posed such danger to all he held dear, nothing was more certain but that the decision he'd made remained his final one. He was going back to that girl and would do everything in his power to help her because although she said she owed it to him, to get away as soon as she could, in actuality *he* owed her, more than she realized and, whatever risks there might be in so doing, it was unthinkable that having come this far, he should break his given word to her without ungainsayable cause. For *other* reasons as well, yes, sure, and there was no sense in denying *those*, either.

What was it that David had said to him the day before? Africa changed people, he'd said, and so it did. For him it had meant, and was meaning, the accelerated ending of idealistic youth, to be replaced by a better understanding of his own weaknesses and strengths never fully tested until now, and of the sort of elemental hunger which, since the opportunity apparently offered, would brook no further procrastination. So yes, that transition was bound to worry him and would affect his attitude to life and work in other and self-rewarding ways as well, maybe, but only if he refused to accept the sometimes questionable compromises which had to be allowed for, as he was beginning to realize, as part of the still unfinished process of growing up.

CHAPTER NINE

The next hour and a half passed with interminable slowness. His mind was obsessed with her — her looks, her plight, her svelte, inviting body — he longed to rejoin her, enjoy her company, her warmth, her sexuality and, if she proved as willing as her behaviour towards him thus far suggested, lay claim to the physical yearning which was his to do with as he pleased. Surely she had made it fairly plain? In other words, she wanted him, equally as much, or nearly so, as he did her before the inevitable and imminent parting of the ways. Of course the very thought of what they had in mind filled him with renewed pangs of doubt and even self-disgust, but those were no more than fleeting deterrents and soon banished, leaving no trace, when confronted with the raw reality of his desire. He had a girl back home who loved him, who had affirmed again and again and on occasion in the past virtually proved she did, whom he was going to marry, and would thus, if he seized his chance now, as he fully intended to do, play false. Apart from that, he ought to remember, the young woman with whom he sought to lie, whose body he coveted, was still a nun and had therefore, presumably, been chaste for years.

Did she recall enough, was *he* man enough, to overcome the inhibitions which they both might well find it very difficult to disregard and be unable to lose themselves in the passion to which they both aspired? Or were they destined to try to give one another pleasure, deep contentment and physical release, but fail, thus making the attempt mental and emotional torture, a travesty, and a descent into an abyss of wasted opportunity, sadness and disillusion? Oh hell — provided she was well enough. Was she? Her back? — it wasn't going to turn out like that, he was convinced, but supposing the images and forebodings which for the moment were plaguing his mind were the products of nothing more than presumption, or wishful thinking, and he'd got it all wrong? Maybe he had. Maybe, truly, he had.

From time to time Nussoula brought people in to see him in his office, sometimes having to stay and explain, or translate, their particular problem or complaint and, almost in a daze, he did his best to concentrate and do his job. He called over to the carpenters' shop not far from the Native Treasury across the road, to take delivery and arrange storage of new furniture for a school soon to be opened down on the Rovum. He had serious words with a recently appointed road foreman who gave every impression of not being up to the work. All these distractions occupied time — it did indeed crawl by — and eventually, by his watch, it was a minute after 5.30. He didn't wait about one second longer, tidied his desk, locking away a confidential file; went out onto the veranda where clerks and uniformed

Messengers were gathering, their day's stint done. He bid them *Kwaheri* and a pleasant evening — warmly reciprocated — before getting into his car and setting off for home. *But then!* Still in third and after driving little more than twenty yards, he trod on the brakes as realization dawned, and drew in to the side of the road.

Because there for all to see — now he came to notice it! — during the course of the day the indefatigable Joseph had done some further work on his vehicle and he now had the carefully mended canopy once more securely in place. He also had doors again, driver's and passenger's side, the latter repaired if not yet repainted, and Joseph had even managed to fit a new piece of perspex instead of the window which had shattered when he'd gone off the road at Mtina. The man was one in a thousand, Benning thought, his gratitude knowing no bounds. Then he was struck suddenly by the fact that, of all the Africans with whom he was in almost daily contact, Joseph was the one about whom he knew least. Where Joseph lived, yes, with a police constable who, like himself, was from the north; his cluttered shed of a workshop not far from the prison compound which Benning had visited often enough, yes also. But as to family, friends, or what he did with such precious little spare time as he chose to allow himself after responding to the many calls upon his probing mind and self-motivated and patient skills — from a *dukawallah*'s wife with a busted flat iron to some kid with a rusting *panga* as well as the general maintenance work and sudden crises of his job, at which he'd never let anyone down and been known to keep on with far into the night — no, about all that background but possibly revealing side of the man's life John Benning realized he knew virtually nothing of any importance. Which wasn't good enough, he decided on the spur of the moment: Joseph Ulaya was, you could say, the new Tanganyika, the one which was soon coming and in the cities had already arrived, and if he, John, aspired to go on fashioning a worthwhile career for himself in this country, as he did, it was individuals of Joseph's stamp — detribalized, ambitious, hardworking and variously skilled — that he'd do well to start getting to know rather better than he did at present. He hadn't come out here, been drawn out here, for Africans of that sort, no — they'd only recently put in an appearance — but perhaps even more crucially than the rural majority they too were surely going to need the understanding and support of committed and far-sighted administrators if, as time went by, they, and the budding unions which represented them, were not to cause all manner of trouble in the future. So, yes —

But, for the moment, he had other things on his mind, and that could wait.

The sun was low, the rutted track wending its way past the DC's bungalow with its cordon of trees overlooking the escarpment, the tang of dry-season Africa — dust, spicy cooking, near-equatorial heat and parched vegetation — in the air through the car windows, with which he was entirely and agreeably familiar. On past the Agricultural Officer's bungalow — he out on safari, as usual — and the high-fenced tennis court much in need of repair. On towards his new bungalow beyond the airstrip and, practically, in the bush and on its own. Because the track deteriorated thereabouts he slowed down a little and changed gear but the sound of his engine was no more than an alien and passing interruption in the enfolding late-afternoon silence which prevailed.

This time there was no one to meet him on the veranda, but his disappointment at that was shortlived as he opened the flyscreen door and entered the sitting-room. He came to a halt in the doorway.

She lay full length on his sofa, to his right: on her back, her head pillowed on the padded armrest nearer to him, her bare feet crossed on the other, and her slim dancer's legs bare to mid-thigh as she'd allowed her sarong — another one of his, as colourful as the first — to ride up in the interest of staying cool. She was sleeping again, but had obviously been reading by the light through the veranda windows behind her; there was an open book, a thriller from his own catholic store, face down on the floor at her side. Her left arm and trailing hand remained close above where she'd put it down, while her right was raised, palm open and long fingers curled, resting on the cushion beside her averted head. He approached very quietly, without disturbing her, a sudden lump in his throat and stood over her, his eyes travelling down the length of her body from head to toe. She was as beautiful and physically desirable to him as any woman who had ever crossed his path; had undone two-three buttons on the shirt of his she wore so that, as she breathed and her chest rose and fell, the outline of her breasts and dark prominent nipples were distinctly revealed beneath their silken near-diaphanous covering. Throttled by emotion, he squatted on his haunches beside her, tempted almost to breaking point to reach out a hand to her naked thighs in a gentle but predatory caress before she was fully awake; run it quickly under the ruckled folds of her sarong, to explore and massage her crotch — but resisted the impulse as so deplorable he could hardly believe he'd had it. He lifted his gaze again to her face. A second or two ago, eyes closed and breathing through parted and pouting lips, she'd apparently been fast asleep, but wasn't now. Eyes alight and wide open, she had turned her head and was smiling at him broadly (and knowingly?) showing her teeth.

All at once she stretched, her whole body tautening, both arms high above her head, her smile changing, and eyeing him without pretence, before she asked softly, "Do I please you?" Not waiting for his reply, she sat up, turned her body and dropped her hands to his neck and shoulders, drew him adamantly towards her so that he went down on one knee and his face was only inches from hers. Gripping her strongly by the upper arms, he held her still, then leaned forward and kissed her expectant mouth; was lost immediately and for long moments in the unconditional response of her lips, teeth and tongue, and any hesitation on his part as to what they were about, which might possibly have made him stop, was abandoned beyond recall. He inserted his left arm beneath her knees, his other round her waist, and rose to his feet, she snuggling against him at once within the compass of his arms.

Carrying her through into the bedroom, he stood her on her feet; swung away to lock the door behind them, while she raised her head and followed his every move with her eyes, as quickly he crossed to the windows and drew the curtains, front and back, so that the light within the room became dimmed and intimate, before returning and confronting her again. Looking down into her face — which gave him look for look, part challenging, part permissive, both irresistible — he began, his hands clumsy, to undo the remaining buttons on her shirt then, parting it, struggled a few moments with the knot holding her sarong in place at the hips. Finally, his teeth gritted and breathing hard, he stripped her naked, letting the two garments she'd been wearing fall to the floor.

"My God, Jeanne, you're lovely," he whispered, in awe at her supple and flawless body, as he took a step back and began to tear at his own clothing to get it off.

"Here, let me," she insisted, and immediately his hands stilled. Stepping forward and frowning in concentration, she undressed him, piece by piece, to the skin; knelt at his feet and untied the laces on his boots; helped him rid himself of boots and socks, also his pants which she'd tugged down round his ankles. Only then did she sit up and reach out with both hands to grip his buttocks and pull him closer; take his already grossly swollen member and balls in trembling fingers, caress and fondle them before — as he bent over her, his hands biting into her shoulders — she introduced his member between her lips and teeth and into her mouth; sucked, pleasured him with her tongue and gently bit him, eyes closed and gulping down her own incontinent saliva — until, groaning softly, he could stand it no more.

Fully aroused as she was by this time, her vagina wet and prehensile, her belly shuddering, their first coupling, on his bed, was both frenzied and uncontrollable; lasted for two minutes only before they came in unison, she writhing and crying out in mounting ecstasy, he ramming into her and ejaculating, on and on, until he was spent. He passed out briefly, and then fell on top of her but she didn't mind, holding him tight, his head against hers, with all the strength she had left. And, in her heart, a joy and satisfaction more than equal to anything she'd ever experienced before.

She was having a shower and trying not to get the pad on her back wet — taking her time and happily reliving as much as she remembered of the past hour. While soaping herself from head to foot and inspecting the bruises he'd given her, which were beginning to show on her left breast, flank and between her thighs, she recalled the savage thrust of his member within her which had left her hotly tumescent and beautifully sore. After their first coitus and he'd had a short rest, he'd been on her and into her *twice* more. Oh God, yes, a young and virile man, long deprived — with sufficient experience to need little prompting — she gave thanks for him and exulted in the knowledge she'd done it, taken and given in love and copulation; had held her own and nothing back. She hadn't forgotten after all the time which had elapsed since years ago.

Remembered enough to pleasure unstintingly a demanding and very well equipped male and rediscover all the physical rapture in exchange which she herself had ever known. By the third time he'd taken her, with her avid co-operation and encouragement, she had been overwhelmed by gratitude to him and totally submissive to their mutual passion and will. Oh God, but he was lovely. She hadn't expected anything like so much and realized wonderingly that she *could* worship him, her saviour made man, given the chance: this young guy who had turned her so quickly into what she thought of as a real woman again. *Bless* him. She wanted to *go on* repaying him for what he'd done, and was doing to her. Couldn't they somehow contrive to have a few more days at least together, before she took off for distant parts? Maybe? She'd have to put it to him, employ all her powers off persuasion, and see. Perhaps, already, he had got her pregnant and, if he had — or even if not — maybe she could use that, after she'd made her escape, to lure him to her once more. To forget him, consign him to history — after today — just wasn't feasible any longer.

After that third time, soaked in sweat, they had fallen into sleep in each other's arms for nigh on half an hour before — leaving her splayed out, naked and exhausted on his bed, in a state of shattered euphoria and still barely conscious — he had left her side, gone to shower and dress again, allowing her all the time she might need to recover and rejoin him when she would. Heavenly it had been, a heavenly time, while slowly she'd gathered herself together, *but* — was he already *regretting* what had happened, now he'd had her? *Was he?* No, please, wasn't that surely unthinkable? She couldn't really believe it; it had been *so* good, but —

Quickly she towelled herself off, and returned to the bedroom, halting beside the bed on which they'd made love; then she whirled and stared at the framed photo on the chest of drawers of his girl — much smaller than the one in his sitting-room and until that moment deliberately ignored. An attractive creature, oh sure — both in the cut of her face and unguarded expression — but how many times had she had him like that? Never, if at all, she was pretty certain. She stepped forward, to turn that girl's eyes and tacit condemnation to the wall, but then stepped, shrugged her shoulders and changed direction, to move across to his almirah, to find herself a fresh shirt of his, another sarong, to replace those cast down on the floor beside the unwanted pillow and crumpled sheet which made up his bedding.

It was while she was selecting what she would wear — standing on one foot because her blistered feet were starting to itch again — that she heard his voice, speaking Swahili, in the adjoining sitting-room. Listened, but couldn't make out what was being said. Could be his trusted servant out there — whom she already thought of, her judgment instinctive, as her ally — but maybe someone else, some stranger, and she knew she had to remain very careful and vigilant or all might yet be lost. So, when she'd found the clean shirt and sarong she wanted and put them on, she went over to the door to the next room and listened again. Salim — the voice she heard answering her recent lover's was definitely his — was actually now taking leave of his employer, it seemed, so, in relief, she gave him time to depart. In a few moments he did, the sound of his sandals crossing the tiled floor to the back door clearly audible. After giving it a little longer, she opened the door quietly and let herself through. Now, John Benning, she thought, what will your first words to me be? Now, in these first seconds of reunion — physical hunger assuaged — how far have we come, or have we regressed? Now that he's had me — and for all the mind-blowing intensity of our mating — is he going to look me in the eye? Or has he had time, come to what he might think of as his senses? Or — what?

Slowly she approached him, her eyes down but occasionally lifted to meet his, in curiosity rather than challenge. Dressed in a lightweight paisley dressing-gown and sandals, he rose from the armchair in which he'd been sitting and awaited her. When she was close and without a word he merely raised and opened his arms to her and welcomed her to him, then enfolded her; held her strongly and possessively against him. In response she put her arms around him and ducked her head, closed her eyes and rested her cheek against his chest. Until suddenly it was all too much for her, his reaction — the love for her and adulation, the sincerity of his emotion which she believed he was striving to convey, more than she deserved in all conscience. Tears of sheer joy welled up inside her and, shaking, she began to weep. Not the weeping kind, she, ever, in normal circumstances; but now, yes, she was unable to hold it in.

He lifted her head then, one hand beneath her chin, and kissed her. She opened her swollen mouth and responded — with all her heart and soul — sobbing on. But then felt herself going weak at the knees; knew she was ready to faint, and tore her face quickly away; hung there in his arms, breathing unevenly and waiting for him to speak.

He said huskily, after a moment, "I was going to have a beer. Jeanne? Will you have one too?"

She straightened up and, still distraught, tried to smile. "A beer, yes," she managed softly, nodding her head. "That would be terrific. I haven't had a beer in donkeys."

He released her, and guided her solicitously to a chair. Unable to look at him, holding on to one of his hands, she lowered herself into it and lay back. He took a clean hanky from the pocket of his robe and offered it to her, and she reached out to take it gratefully. Used it on cheeks and eyes — then blew her nose — recovering her composure with an effort of will which left her breathless. Watched him as he crossed to the fridge beyond the dining-table, opened it, and bent to look inside.

She found her voice again, and asked, "That was — that was Salim I heard you talking to, just now?"

"Yes," he said, turning, a couple of bottles of San Mig beer in his hands, before he nudged the door closed again with his elbow. "It slipped my mind, but this is his night off and he'll soon be gone, taking the boy — who's a relative of his — with him." And he explained further, "He's building a bigger house for himself and his family on the south side of town and he goes down there to see how the *fundi* working on it is getting on, give him fresh instructions and so forth. Then he sleeps the night at his old place, returning before lunchtime tomorrow."

Smiling up at him across the room, and his hanky now balled in her fist, she queried, "So how will we manage for supper tonight? Shall I cook something? What do you usually do?"

"He'll leave us some cold food before he goes, I expect," Benning said. "He'll bring it in a moment and put it on the table." Halting by the sideboard, he began uncapping bottles with an opener, then pouring their contents into tall glasses, looking across at her and adding, "So the place is ours this evening," and, with a touch of diffidence, "Personally, I couldn't ask for anything better."

"Me too," she said, in unqualified approval. "Oh yes, that's fine with me."

He finished what he was doing and came to her; gave a glass into her hand. Then he retreated to sit one end of the sofa, saying, "Come over here beside me, will you, Jeanne?" and he patted the other end of the sofa with his free hand, before tucking in the two halves of the dressing-gown he was wearing a little more decorously to cover his bare legs.

She rose at once and sat down again at his side, her glass consigned to a low stool; edged closer so her hip was in intimate contact with his. He put his arm round her waist and, after a moment, asked, "How's the back? I'm afraid I —"

"Haven't given it a thought in hours," she said, not strictly truthfully. She rested her head against his shoulder and her hand on his thigh. "Your pad didn't come off while we — so it has to be OK, I think. It's stuck a little in a couple of places, that's all."

"I'll have a look at it again later, if you'd like me to," he said and, at her murmur of assent, raised his glass and, striving to say something to her a great deal more important than that and in search of adequate words, looked away. She reached out for her glass also, and waited for him. Eventually he said, "I can't begin to tell you, but please believe me, I never in my life — I never imagined —"

"Don't go on," she said quietly. "Because it was no different for me, I promise you." She shut her eyes and bit her lip. "I wanted to hold you and give to you, until I dropped, and it took me by surprise. It's been that way for me before, once, but I was still only a teenager then, and I never suspected —"

"I adore you," he said. "It's not merely . . . You make me feel very humble and strong — very lucky to be a man. Thank you, from my heart." And, raising his glass a little higher, he concluded, "Cheers, my love, you darling wonderful girl. Here's to us."

"To *you*," she corrected. "You were here, you let me stay, and since I came —" But she didn't say more, blinking a couple of times and shaking her head. After touching glasses, they settled back into the sofa together, and drank, "Wow, that's pretty nice, I'd forgotten," she remarked, licking her lips and looking down into her glass. "Never mind it'll probably go straight to my head. Brings back memories, though, indeed it does."

"Good ones?" he asked.

"Some good, some I could do without," she admitted, and left it there.

He wasn't certain she fully understood, even now; to assure her he was with her *unconditionally* from this time on — anything else was unimaginable — but heard footsteps mounting then crossing the stoep at the back of the house, so reluctantly withdrew his arm from around her and awaited Salim's arrival. A big tray in his hands, his servant halted in the doorway before coming in and, not looking at them directly, set his tray down on the dining table behind them. Came round to them after that and told them what he'd brought: hard-boiled eggs and sliced bully-beef, potato salad, lettuce from the prison gardens; fresh fruit to follow plus a slab of cheese, a loaf of bread and tinned butter — all protected from flies beneath mosquito-net umbrellas. Finally he salaamed, glancing down at them for a second, it appeared with real affection, and said, "*Nakwenda sasa*, bwana, *memsaab*" — I'm going now. If you wish to make tea, coffee, later, the stove in the kitchen's still hot, or I can fill you a flask of boiling water before I go."

"No need, *baba*, thank you," Benning said. "We'll get it ourselves, if we want it. You take off now." And he added, "Hope all's going well with the new house and your *fundi*'s doing his stuff."

Shaking his head ruefully, Salim said, "He's a Makua" — a nomadic tribe from the south-east of Longoro District with a dubious reputation — "so I have to keep an eye on him. Which I do." And, with that, he salaamed again and took his leave.

After he'd gone, Jeanne said, "Seems a very good man, that. You're extremely lucky to have him."

"I think so too," Benning said. "But, apart from anything else, he likes you, I can tell. He thinks you're the best thing that's happened to me since he came here to work."

"And you?" she asked softly. "Is that what you think, as well? Is he right?"

"Oh God, yes," Benning said. But then, turning to her, he went on curiously, "But what was it, my love, that made you come *to me*? Did you have some plan of escape which involved myself from the start?"

She didn't answer at once; rested her head against the back of the sofa and closed her eyes. Concentrated her mind and thought over where they stood, as of now, and all that had occurred with such rapidity since her arrival. And realized that the idea she'd had in the beginning, of using him to further her own cynical ends, had lost all relevance; was indeed repulsive to her after everything that had taken place between them less than an hour ago. That now, out of the blue, so it felt, she revered and loved him — had fallen for him, in truth — and the thought of hurting him, damaging him, his career, by using him, had become anathema to her. It wasn't that simple any more. She wanted now to *stay* with him as of right, become his woman and part of his life — if they could possibly bring it about — *that*, above anything else. But was aware also that, in reality, she was only crying for the moon. Supposing she did persuade him to allow her to stay, as she believed she could, news of her presence here, her continuing presence, was bound to get out and it would happen sooner rather than later. And effectively she *would* destroy him then. Not only that but she herself would fall once more into the clutches of those who would have no sympathy with her at all, she feared: certainly not in condoning let alone understanding the change in her life's orientation which had overtaken her out at Mtina that night and the day following. In fact they'd probably do everything in their power to talk her out of it, thus making of her existence a desperate struggle for personal survival which, in the end, she might not be strong enough to win. So no, she had to think and act long term. It saddened her unmercifully to envisage an impending period of self-denial and deprivation, but she must: plead for his assistance in getting away, *tonight!* Once she'd made it out of the country, as she damn well would then, she would keep in touch with him, woo him from afar, in the hope . . . in the hope that — And in the hours left to them give him plenty to remember her by, plenty, *more*.

"Sorry, so sorry," she said and, opening her eyes again, she sat forward, glass in hand. Raising it she took a sip, before adding, "I had to think things through."

"And?" he asked.

To be honest with him? Yes, she wanted him to know now, whatever risks it might entail, not only her body which already he'd pleasured to the very limits of all she could take, and hopefully would soon do so again, but her sometimes illogical, too often impatient mind as well: to put their commitment to one another to the test, being confident by this time — overconfident, maybe? — that if he saw her as she really was, without illusion, warts and all, and she was reading him aright, it was only likely to intensify his infatuation with her, curiosity about her and desire to explore her further, 'til her soul lay bare, just as it was becoming her ambition to possess his. It was an aspiration, call it a compulsion, too fundamental and enticing to deride; one of the remembered paradoxes of requited love and, in the long run, she passionately suspected, if she wished to make him her own over time and for ever, as all at once she was determined to do, there was no alternative. She could only pray he had the maturity and singlemindedness to match her own and hope for the best. So, all or nothing creature as she tended to be and her mind made up, she asked, apparently inconsequentially, "How far is it to Mingida?"

"Mingida? he said wonderingly. "A hundred and sixty miles, more than four hours" drive, at least. Why?"

"Isn't there a long-distance bus from there run by Tanganyika Railways which goes once or twice a week to Mbeya in the Southern Highlands, and then on north to Dodoma, where one can take the train to Dar-es-Salaam?"

"Yes, I believe so," he said.

"And isn't it a proper service with comfortable coaches which are well maintained and don't break down, or, if they do, a replacement bus is despatched straightaway?"

"So I've heard," he agreed.

"That was what I planned to do, from the outset," she said. She turned to grin at him, her eyes gleaming. "Get to you and, when I'd done that, seduce you — you're quite a dish, you know, and I didn't think it would involve too much hardship — after that, as soon as you were besotted with me —"

"I *am* besotted," he murmured, interrupting her. "Go on."

"As soon as that was accomplished, then I'd prevail on you to drive me to Mingida, put me on the bus, pay my fare, lend me some cash and so forth because, of course, I don't have a cent. Following which I fully intended to forget you without a qualm or backward glance. It didn't bother me one bit that you could quite easily get into serious trouble, even lose your job, if what you'd done became known, as it well might — while I beat it out of the country, by air from Dar, and was never heard of again."

"You have your passport?" he asked. Shocked, he supposed, taken aback and disappointed by her candour and openness, the ruthless amorality of her intentions *vis-à-vis* himself which, thus far, she'd made no attempt to play down. At the same time . . .

"No, you don't need a passport for Kenya," she said.

"But after Kenya?" he persisted.

"By bus again, across the border and into the Congo. There, who knows?" she conceded, frowning a little. "But, given any luck, I'd be able to work something out."

He was silent for a full minute, taking it in. But then he said quietly, "Crazy, Jeanne. Really, madness." The

Congo part of it, especially, was surely a step beyond the bounds of feasibility and acceptable risk. But if she were serious, as he believed she was, he knew himself torn between a grudging admiration for a daredevil kind of courage — rare in a woman? — and suspicions of a naïvety and foolhardiness so ungovernable as to cast a doubt or two upon her sanity. And yet? And yet? Did that mean he should try to stop her? Refuse to help her? Try to persuade her to think again? Failing that, hand her over to the very people she was bent on getting away from, for probably good reason, and thereby save his own skin? No, whatever else might be on the cards he wasn't prepared to do that, not any more. He'd find it very difficult to forgive himself, afterwards, if he did. Besides which, her defiant fortitude as already revealed by her long march to his door and near-blatant reliance on her own physical and sexual prowess to get her own way, filled him with a timeless if somewhat wary respect. Woman? Yes, *this* was woman, of a kind to scare the hell out of a man or, conversely, pull out all the stops, with her and for her, and by so doing prove himself (to himself).

He rose to his feet. Outside it was beginning to get dark as night fell, and very thoughtfully he crossed to the back door; closed it and drew the curtains before, hearing the station generator thudding away in the distance across the airstrip, he switched on some lights. He went over to the fridge and returned to her with a fresh bottle of San Mig in hand; reprimed her glass when she held it out to him. Standing over her, and she looking up at him quizzically and in silence, he said,

"You've told me what your original plan was, is that right? So it's changed now, has it?"

"No, it's not changed," she said, slowly shaking her head. "But the ending's different."

"In what way?" he asked, resuming his seat beside her. "You have to tell me." In the partly lit room the silence was total except for their quiet breathing. They drank together again, and then she bowed her head, holding her glass in her lap.

"I would like to stay on here now, with you," she said, then went on, not seeking to conceal her pain, "but I know I mustn't do that; it would ruin you, and that's the last thing I want any longer. I'd like to share your life here, go with you everywhere, be here for you when you return from the office, or safari, so that my love for you has time to deepen and grow and our mutual lust for one another's bodies has the chance to express itself in all the ways which take our fancy —"

"Don't, Jeanne," he whispered. "Please, don't."

"No," she said, "all right, I won't. I'm not going to give up, though, but I realize now I have to be patient. Wait for you, far away, in the hope you'll not forget me, and then come to me when your tour of duty's done, so we can be together again. Six months, I think you said, six months of purgatory, longing and memories, until I can be sure, one way or the other. But it will pass, of course it will, and in that time I will write to you, beg you, remind you of all we've shared so far, send my love and constancy to you halfway across the world." Suddenly and with little warning she shuddered and broke down; couldn't go on. Put her glass aside with a stifled moan and huddled over her knees to hide her face, clutching at her cheeks with trembling hands.

He leaned over her, head lowered, and drew her across his lap; murmured reassurance and promises in her ear, trying to convince her and get her to accept that she had nothing to fear." For the time being, anyway, nothing. Finally, gripping her shoulders, he raised her until she was sitting upright again, her face turned from him, mouth gaping and cheeks wet with tears. He made her look at him, wide-eyed, and kissed her, one arm holding her to him, the other fondling her breasts until, in the agony and exultation of urgent desire, they collapsed again into the sofa together.

She tore her face away then and slipped out of his embrace. In one lithe unexpected movement she slid forward off the sofa, knelt and turned before him, positioning herself and separating his knees with her hands. She insinuated her shoulders and torso between them, tossed aside the two halves of his dressing-gown to get at his groin. Tormented and manipulated his balls and naked member with impassioned loving fingers, and when he was fully aroused, rose and undid her sarong, letting it fall to the floor. Sat astride him, knees gripping him above the waist while, leaning over him and supporting herself on the back of the sofa with one hand, with the other — by feel alone and smiling distantly — she guided him into her.

CHAPTER TEN

They drove through the night, westwards, along the Mingida road. It was one o'clock in the morning of the following day, one of the two days in the week according to a recent timetable he had in his desk, under the window in his spare room, on which the long-distance bus was scheduled to leave Mingida for Dodoma at 10a.m.

Back at the house they had spent a laughing, often naked, sexually intimate and licentious evening together. They had eaten a good meal between times, and split a bottle of Aphroditi, before sleeping together for four hours, exhausted, in one another's arms. On being woken by his alarm, they made love again, got up, showered and drowsily dressed; made ready for departure. His Land Rover stood waiting not far from the front door; to it he transferred the two four-gallon cans of petrol he always kept in reserve in his garage and stowed them in the back. Together they then prepared cheese and pickle sandwiches, also big flasks of sweet tea and coffee; filled a couple of 2-litre canteens with drinking water from the filter. After that he sat down at the table and, with her standing beside him, her hand on his shoulder, composed a note to

David Morgan explaining his absence, and to be delivered by Nussoula — night watchman at the District Office that week — in the morning, saying that report had reached him of a potentially explosive inter-village fracas out at Nampungu on the Langoro/ Mingida border, and that he was going out there to investigate, send for back-up if necessary, and generally do what he could to calm things down, hopefully to return the following afternoon. Later, he could always say he'd got there to find the problem either overdramatized or already amicably sorted out so intervention on his part, therefore, unnecessary, which ought to take care of any queries which might subsequently arise. Finally, prior to their departure, and perhaps of greater importance than anything else, he unlocked a drawer in his almirah and transferred to his wallet all the cash he had there — nearly a thousand shillings in notes — then took out his chequebook and the most recent statement he'd received, less than a fortnight ago, from his bank in Lindi. There being little to spend his money on at Langoro, this showed a healthy balance of nearly £1,500 from accrued salary plus allowances, and he was confident he'd be able to draw on this at the one bank there was at Mingida which, by good fortune and sound banking sense was a branch of the same one he'd patronized in Lindi since his arrival in Africa. He could then provide her with her bus and train fares north, plus a considerable sum to assist her on her way thereafter.

But those things attended to they didn't leave immediately, while knowing in their hearts they might well be wasting what could turn out to be valuable time. It seemed important to them not to rush away from this house at which they had first discovered one another and in which their love for each other — driven by physical hunger, deprivation and longing — had grown until it had taken over their world. They were suddenly both soberingly sad — six months was a dreadfully long time — and they sat at the dining-table, their hands clasped across it, in silence and heads bowed, taking leave of one another during a long five minutes of prayer and introspection the opportunity for which they couldn't expect to recur before they reached Mingida and she would be away and gone.

Abruptly she rose to her feet, shaking her head, and said, "All right, let's do it. Let's go," and, turning full circle, her head lifted and arms outspread, she sang out with an attempt at gaiety, "Goodbye, house, and thank you for everything. See you again one day, maybe, and until I return, let my presence live on here and remind your master of all he means to me. Don't let him forget, please, don't let him forget." And, with that, dropping her arms and beckoning to him, her eyes moist, she strode to the front door and held it open for him to precede her outside.

He had one last thing to do, though, and, gesturing apology to her, went to fetch his handgun, his cased Luger — the parting present from his father — plus a box of ammunition from the drawer in his bedside table. You never knew, and to have it with them in the coming hours just might prove of incalculable importance.

When he came out to her again, she glanced at what he was carrying, under his arm, but made no comment, and together, by torchlight, they went out into the dark.

The night was still and a three-quarter moon high in the sky above the speeding vehicle, the raised dust of their passing swirling and settling behind them. The road ahead was wide and adequately graded, a broad trace pale, sometimes gravelly and gleaming in the path of their single headlight. For the most part it was as straight as a survey line between the mass of escorting undergrowth beneath thorny acacia but also occasional taller jungle trees. In their depths the eyes of nocturnal animals were reflected and shone out from time to time, watching them go by, and once or twice they caught sight of a nighthawk on the hunt, crossing the road ahead at treetop height. No people were about at this hour — much too dangerous — and the villages they drove through at intervals showed not a glimmer of light. They had the world, the Continent of Africa, to themselves and, especially in the pockets of mist in which they were compelled to slow down, it was undoubtedly a little eerie.

They spoke hardly at all above the noise of the engine, sometimes holding hands on the seat between them. Then, after about an hour, she withdrew and curled herself into her corner, shut her eyes, and drifted away into sleep.

She awoke with a start twenty minutes later and, for half a minute, found it difficult to remember where she was and what she was doing here, travelling an unfamiliar road through the night. Then, as memory returned, physical awareness, and she made out the indistinct profile of the driver, sitting braced, his hands on the steering-wheel at her side, it all came back to mock her, and make her think: yes, she had loved him, thrilled at his touch and power to move her, the effect she'd had on him until she was sensually assuaged, played out, aching and sore, and had had it all. It had been a time of rediscovery and emotional intoxication, never, ever, to be forgotten, *but* — but there were other men, many, who would find her attractive and beddable, *he* had confirmed that to her, and a world in which it would be fascinating to make her way. *Outside* Africa — back "home" — that was the crucial point. She had had enough of Africa, more than enough, she realized, and had no desire to return. To what? A lonely existence on isolated bush stations for many years, deprived of his love-making and company for long periods when he was out on safari, with little or nothing to do and, if she became pregnant, the prospect of giving birth in some distant clinic probably with third-rate amenities, and at the mercy of barely qualified practitioners? No, not a pleasant thought; in fact a very daunting one. Besides, she had no desire at all for babies; she wanted, now that she was close to attaining it, *life* in its fullest sense, meaning cities, people of her own race and kind, to pick and choose from, encounter and mingle with, the shops, the cinemas, the sport, the diversity; the same life, only better because she'd appreciate it more, as the one she'd grown up with, been part of and thrived on until that cruel and catastrophic event long ago. No, not the sort of life she was ever likely to find with the man beside her, in the wastes and primitive conditions of Africa.

Just beyond Nampungu, they stopped for coffee and to stretch their legs at the roadside, and she allowed him to fondle and caress her, and responded in kind because she owed him and, truly, he turned her on. Also she was aware that she must *not* give him the smallest hint of the direction in which her thoughts were leading her. To use him, his love, his cash — as she had planned to do from the start — because it was necessary if she were to have the slightest chance of making it — out. After that gradually — or immediately? — break off all contact with him — no letters, no answering cables, nothing — while fully intending, as soon as she could, to reimburse him for the considerable sums of money he was shortly going to shell out. Yes, she would do that, and must, or her conscience would never permit her any peace, thereafter.

So out — and goodbye — sure, and in this particular way, via Mingida which, back at the mission, she herself had chosen very much in keeping with her temperament, she acknowledged, and which still excited her, its many challenges no doubt yet to come. But back there her tormented mind had been principally occupied, even obsessed, by the lure of getting away, in the first instance, *to him*: what happpened after she'd made him her own, while an integral part of her overall plan, and in her imagination perfectly feasible, had been of secondary importance, to be faced and tackled in detail when the time came. As it now had, and with it the realization, beginning to give her pause, that in a matter of hours the die would be irrevocably cast and she would be alone again: the hardest part of her flight to a different future barely begun and nearly all still to do. Truly that was a bit scary suddenly — if far too late in the day, she upbraided herself, to allow her the foolishness and gutlessness of second thoughts — but there was no sense in denying their emergence all the same, and she didn't try.

However, she kept her incipient misgivings entirely to herself and permitted no trace of them to show while they were having their short breather together at the side of the road and, as soon as they were rested a little, they drove on and across the border, marked by a peeling and roughly painted sign, into Mingida District. They still had eighty miles to go.

It was while they were climbing the gentle slopes into the Kilimande hills beyond the border — their rolling summits, if you could call them that, never more than 500 feet high — that he began to be afflicted by doubts. To begin to wonder. Whether, after getting her out of the country successfully, he *really* wanted this girl beside him to come back, as his wife. Apart from her pliant, rapacious and sex-starved body which had enchanted him until his whole life seemed to centre on the next time he'd be able to partake of her again, what did he know of her? Not much that gave him confidence for the future. That for six years she had been a nun, the sort who had welcomed and encouraged the brutal scourging of her body when she felt she'd transgressed and merited punishment, which had caused her, in reaction, to repudiate and disavow whatever all those six years had meant to her and had set out to make up for time lost. So what was to stop her, when the mood took her at some time in the future and she no longer on heat, doing precisely the same thing, or something like it, in reverse? What had happened out at Mtina that night — and since, for that matter — had been the product of an unbalanced and fevered mind, had it not? A mind, coupled with a long-repressed physical ardour, so unstable, masochistic and uncontrollable that, with her around, there could never be any surety or long term peace.

This brought up in his mind, for the first time in many hours, the image and beguiling memory of his girl, Elizabeth, who was sexy enough too and who, until twenty-four hours ago he'd fully expected to wed and settle down with in marital bliss for the rest of his life. Suddenly the thought of hurting her deeply — as he would — abandoning her in favour of a lascivious, alluring maybe, but plainly unpredictable hetaira was more than he could bear to contemplate and took him a long way towards a decision not to let it come about. She, the hetaira, had caught him at a time when sexual hunger was hounding him almost beyond endurance, as happened to young, virile expatriate males in many parts of Africa, instances of its often wretched consequences being widely reported. She had taken full advantage of his predicament, and her own, but that was insufficient reason to throw away all the few certainties in relation to the opposite sex he'd ever had up till now. That didn't mean, however, that he was going to rid himself of this girl beside him as soon as he could. No, if he did, she could still damage him for some while, even ruin his career and forthcoming marriage, apart from the consideration that to do so — after all that had passed between them, which had granted him an unforgettable interlude of sexual indulgence and euphoria — would be a dastardly and unforgivable way to behave. Ashamed, as he was beginning to be of betraying his fiancée back home at the first real opportunity, given that African girls were untouchable, he still owed this other at his side more even than she actually knew and would never find it acceptable should he not do everything in his power to repay her. It wasn't going to be easy, though, to hide his intentions from her in the few hours they had left. He knew that as well, but somehow he'd have to contrive to do it.

Still in the hills they drove through a big village whose name he didn't know, with a signed Posts and Telegraphs office at the roadside and a couple of obvious cantinas, catering to long-distance travellers, both closed. It was now five o'clock in the morning, dawn and daylight in the offing, and they had made good time: hadn't much more than forty miles of their long journey left. In Mingida only three things needed to be done before her departure: get to the bank as soon as it opened at eight and arrange finance; seek out one or other of the two big *dukas* which sold European women's clothing and let her pick out what she wanted, plus a few toiletries, also a suitcase in which to carry her gear; finally find the bus terminus and purchase her ticket. They'd have a couple of hours at least in the town before their time was up, and surely that would be ample; either way there was no point in getting there too early. So he suggested stopping for breakfast and told her that, in any case, they'd better fill up the *gari* with petrol.

She said yes, why not, she wouldn't mind a drink and a bite to eat, also needed a pee, so — after descending into an extensive, apparently treeless and mostly barren valley — he pulled up beside a shallow running stream and switched off. He sat back and undid a couple of buttons on his shirt, closed his eyes a second or two to rest them, before glancing across at her, a little warily. She opened her door, and stepped down lightly; paused a moment, working her shoulders and stretching, looking round; then she disappeared round the back for two minutes before reappearing and going along the bonnet a little way until he could see her better, where she turned expectantly, waiting for him to join her. Bareheaded, a scarf round her throat, wearing a shirt of his tucked into her long skirt, which was belted at the waist, she was — with her dark, flashing-eyed good looks and sensational figure — as seriously beautiful a woman as he'd ever known, and it amazed him, humbled him, that a woman so gifted had recently, and so memorably, consented to and enthusiastically participated with him in acts of passion both conventional and erotically bizarre — many at her instigation and way beyond his previous experience —

not far removed, indeed, from the wilder of his sexual fantasies. He was overcome by regret that he and she must end — mustn't they? — very soon, this morning, and that he would never see her, lie with her, again. But it doesn't have to be like that, does it, he thought. I can resign from the service, I'm young and highly qualified; I can find another similar job quite easily and then together we can set out to take our chances in another part of the world. But no, just no, that wasn't on, and he knew that too. He wasn't brave enough, for one thing, a perception which filled him with a certain surprise. Either that, or too sensible. He *was* in love with this job he had, a good one in which he might expect to rise to the top eventually; in love also and in thrall to Africa, its harsh obligations, hard-earned rewards, wonderful scenery, animal life and diverse peoples. The idea of leaving for parts unknown appealed to him as little as unwarranted martyrdom. So no, he'd seek to avoid that at almost any price, which meant, in the fullness of time Elizabeth would join him out here, *she*, and, in tandem, they'd go forward along paths which, given good fortune and dedication, would lead to lives both personally fulfilling and of service to an ideal.

Except! Except he wasn't too sure whether Elizabeth was either ready or equipped to cope with Africa. A thought which had occurred to him, and been dismissed as of secondary importance, at odd times before. She was a city girl and, for all his detailed, informative and optimistic descriptions in letters, didn't really have much of an idea of what she would be letting herself in for in places like Langoro. Neither did she have the language, or any previous experience of Africans. Even in the limited time he had spent out here he had encountered, sadly, too many *memsaabs* who were fairly obviously bitter, miserable with their lot, and regretted deeply their decision to follow their man into the frightening embrace of what now seemed manifestly to them a dark continent. This led — again obviously enough, as in Patti and David Morgan's case — to strife at home, unhappiness, sexual infidelity and often otherwise proficient administrators going through the motions of doing their jobs when, given the support they needed from a composed and loving spouse, they were capable of a great deal more. And who suffered for that in the long run? Africans, of course, most of whom deserved men of principled determination, unsullied conviction, humanity and undiminished self-confidence to advance and give them a lead.

Which brought him again to that girl standing out there at the roadside, illuminated by the lights of his car. She might have been a nun and undoubtedly had an all too human unstable and self-destructive streak, but *she* had the language, she knew Africa, and had actually worked successfully with African women. She had had dealings with their menfolk as well across a difficult religious, sometimes pagan, divide, and was aware of the pitfalls. *She* already knew the bush and bush stations, and what to expect; also something at least of what his job required of him. More than that, given her gender, training and experience as a teacher, she could actually help him, if she wanted to, and quickly become an indispensable collaborator in the growing welfare side of his work. All qualifications which Elizabeth, who had beavered away in an estate agent's office since leaving college, simply did not possess. So there she was, Jeanne, a different calibre of girl and she made him think seriously, again. If she *were* to become part of his life, for both their sakes he'd have to ask for a transfer from Langoro to another station in the north where her history, should it become known, could well be adjudged either immaterial or a closed book. He knew, felt it in his bones, that in order to have her love, unleashed sexuality and guts, the regret which might temporarily afflict him at leaving Langoro behind him for ever wouldn't be a price he'd find too much difficulty in paying. A transfer, sure, if he asked for one it was a near certainty he'd get it; young DOs, especially those with a promising future, were always being shuffled about whether they liked it or not. It improved their competence and broadened their horizons. So why not? It could be done like that, because he was captivated, enamoured as never before. He wanted her, *that* above anything else: the sexual attraction between them felt like the unfettering of uncontrollable twin forces of nature, not to mention the hidden tides of ultimate destiny — following which, once achieved, they'd be together. For the rest of time, God willing,

So — Sorry, Elizabeth, so very sorry, my erstwhile love: you were grand; you were all I thought I'd ever want, and at times out here memories of you and the promises you made kept me sane, for which I can never thank you enough, but you don't really compare, I have to say. No, not, and that's the truth. Believe me, I wish so much —

Taking the torch, he got down and went round the back of the Land Rover; let down the tailgate and pulled out her leather satchel in which they'd stowed most of their supplies and took it round the front of the vehicle. Aware, as he did so, that the decision he'd come to but a minute or two ago filled him with a certain remorse, perhaps, but also an unarguable and joyous sense of relief.

Restless, she had moved away from the car a few steps, but turned and saw him coming: at first only a shadow moving then, as he rounded the bonnet into the full glare of the headlight, her heart lurched and she caught her breath, at the sight of him: the personificattion in her eyes — why deny it? — of virile youth and male beauty. She was momentarily stricken, both physically and emotionally because, as a man, without doubt, by his mere appearance and personal magnetism — as a reason for the physical dialogue which she had initiated but which had overwhelmed them both, been explored and made their own, just a very few hours ago — he possessed the power to destroy her will. Shivering and bewildered, wide-eyed and unable to get a word out, she continued to watch him while he leaned over the satchel on the bonnet. His blond hair tousled, his rangy athletic build which she vividly recalled in all its naked symmetry and muscular perfection, was set off so well by the outfit he wore, a sweat-stained bush shirt, neckerchief, khaki trousers and desert boots. She wanted to run to him, caress and arouse him again, offer herself and her body; implore him to take her once more and, should he do it brutally, mercilessly, even tear her, so what? She'd scream and fight, but submit, and treasure every minute of it, rapturously, however far he went. It had never, but never, happened to her before in anything approaching the same way, with such emboldening and frantic insistence. Or, if it had, something like it, six long years ago, she didn't want to remember it. To covet a particular man so much and desire to humble and sacrifice herself, her pride and all pretence, for him — a second time — was more than she'd bargained for, or believed attainable, either in this, or any other world.

Shakily she folded at the knees and settled on the hard ground, propping herself up on one hand and arm; went on staring up at him as, smiling across at her, he set out their food from the satchel on the bonnet. Thinking, in a shattered sort of way; latching on to thoughts as they entered her mind and accepting the decisions which followed at once as if there were no other options open to her, none that stood the remotest chance. Though there might be other men back home, a different, even fuller and more exciting life, she wanted none of it, or them. Only to stay with him, wherever he was, even in Africa; be there for him, love him, serve him in every sense and keep him by her side. Nothing else mattered, only that, and it came as a revelation to her. Oh sure, he'd have to get a transfer and she'd have to wait maybe six months, but then, after that, *then*. And she'd be able to help him in his work, wouldn't she? Become a partner in an active sharing sort of way to all he did. And when she became pregnant by him, God willing, those babies would be *his* and *hers*, not some second-choice and as yet unidentified stranger's, and that made all the difference. She would endure any hardship, take every risk, willingly, in pursuit of so ravishing a denouement. Because in confirmation and entire justification for her sudden change of heart, she remembered viscerally again, the occasion, back at his bungalow at Langoro, there had come a time, nearing the end of a bout of steamy and wordless intercourse between them before supper, that he had her pinned down on her front across his bed, his fingers deep into and goading gently that part of her body she'd hours ago given him as a present — while, gasping and distraught, her elbow crooked, she made free with his softening prick and balls — when he had shifted his body a little and lowered his head; begun to kiss and follow with his lips, very tenderly, the lines of half-healed and still itching stripes across her back from the whipping she'd undergone but four nights since, the pad with which he'd covered and doctored them long since detached and vanished without trace. And, at his touch in that particular way, both grieving and reverent with a leavening of guilt thrown in, she had gone limp and boneless, weeping, suspecting she existed for one reason only: to *die* for him — as years ago someone else had died at her hands — and wished for long distracted moments, before she snapped out of it, he would actually ask that of her so she could dutifully and eagerly comply. It had been then she had first come close to understanding the extent and nature of her indebtedness to him, she supposed, that with him, and for him, she could put that terrible event in her past behind her for ever, but hadn't appreciated it so clearly at the time.

Breathing hard, her eyes fey, she clambered to her feet and went towards him where he stood pouring tea from a flask and, as she approached, tore open the buttons of the shirt of his she wore to reveal her naked breasts. Gripped his hands fiercely as he turned and extended them to her, and bent forward, to lower and thrust her breasts and aching nipples into his enfolding grasp. She stared at him, challenged him as she straightened up and unbuckled her belt, began to wriggle out of the skirt which confined her belly and lower limbs; saying softly, "Johnny-love, I'm your woman. Please take me, one last time, and never forget, my darling, never for one second forget, *me*."

So he did, the car door open and she leaning back, legs wide and on tiptoe, against the cushioned front seat, and this final coupling of theirs — she moaning and crying out, coming on to him, while he whispered his panting endearments — was almost unbearably poignant and possessive: ratification of an agreement between man and woman arrived at irrevocably on both sides, in absolute certainty. When together and in private, in bed or out, they'd never be able to keep their hands off each other for long, they knew that now. By using hands and bodies to speak their minds — there being no *time* for words — express their love and interdependence to the full by way of liking it rough as well as smooth, which said a lot, and to deny all that a senseless rejection of a Godgifted natural phenomenon, an insatiable physical and emotional compatability discovered and, it felt, preordained. Of course, and she knew this from memory and experience better than he, in time the white heat of their passion for one another would settle down into a slow-burn of visual and tactile intimacy, nights of bodily communion and protracted waking — these punctuated on occasion by a return to the wilder shores of sexual confrontation when their sensual rhythms coincided to urge it upon them, or in loving and compulsive response to the other's perceived and importunate need. Christ, yes, she thought: all that was to be expected and longingly looked forward to as well, a whole lifetime of it yet to come, *but* — But so much now depended on the next few days and weeks, on how she fared, in the course of this journey before her, her flight out — and what happened and lay in store for her *en route*.

She had to get home now, safely; she *must*.

CHAPTER ELEVEN

As dawn was breaking under heavy night-cloud to the east, they drove on, still in the hills but in jungle-country again. The shadowy half-lit trees an avenue ahead, overhanging branches, some low, picked out in the fullness of leaf by the lights, and their dust-cloud behind them merging quickly into the mist. Then a village and cultivation either side of the road: people stirring out with cloths around their heads and throats, mangy dogs — then jungle once more.

He drove one-handed most of the time and held her to him as she snuggled against him, resting her head against his shoulder. Silent, and tired again, their time — this time — was nearly over and the sense of imminent and near-unbearable loss which they knew would afflict them in full force as soon as he'd seen her seated on her bus and waved it off as it disappeared into the distance, northwards, was already getting its claws into them and tormenting them with the prospect of loneliness and long months of separation.

But there were still things he ought to know and, after a few miles, he asked quietly, "Where will you go, back home, when you get there?" Because surprisingly they hadn't got round to speaking of that before, and he felt he should have some idea of what her plans for the foreseeable future might be.

"To my sister's," she murmured, "in Harrogate. That's where I left a few things. We don't get on too well, we never have, but it's a place to start. I'll find a place of my own and some sort of job as soon as I can."

That she had a tidy sum of money in her name, invested in Post Office Savings, which she'd be able to draw on, or use as collateral, shortly after her arrival in Britain, she'd already confided to him prior to their departure from Langoro, so her ability to support herself until she'd settled in didn't worry him unduly. But it was in *getting* there — across a vast continent, and then on — given the difficulties which were bound to crop up, the real dangers she might well have to face on the way, alone, and for all her courage and (unthinking?) self-confidence, those worried him very much. Indeed they did. She had to leave — there was nothing else for it — and had set out to do it like this; initially she'd have his cash, every penny he could lay hands on, but —

"I'm beginning to be afraid, you know," she conceded, into his shoulder. "I wasn't afraid before. I saw all that lies ahead like some exciting adventure. Whatever turned up I'd manage somehow, but I'm not as sure about it now as I was, no, I'm not." And she added, pressing against him, "I've so much more to lose now than ever I thought."

What to say to revive her previously dauntless but now faltering resolution and audacity? She was going to need both! Restore the faith, stop-at-nothing intransigence and singleness of purpose which had characterized her every move from the outset and on which she'd have to rely in the days and weeks to come? No doubt such faith — given luck, quick-thinking and bloodymindedness — could move mountains, ease her path and overcome most obstacles. At the same time, and especially if her nerve deserted her, it could also lead her straight into the jaws of disaster! So, even at this eleventh hour, should he think again about his commitment to get her away by this route as far too risky and problematical and insist on taking her back to Langoro? But if he did, they would lose too much, maybe everything — it was virtually a certainty — and in addition she might well see it as betrayal and end up despising him. For those reasons, truly, no, there could be no going back anymore. It was a little like being caught in a trap of their own devising, he thought, with no way out, only to pray that the daring and fortitude of which she was capable — and for which he loved her — stayed with her, or returned to carry her through in time of need or danger, against the odds. So, faced with one last possible chance of changing the course of events for better or worse, he ducked it. Couldn't bring himself to say no, this wasn't on, even supposing she'd listen, which was highly unlikely — lay it on the line to her and *then do it*, whatever she might say, in the overriding interest of ensuring she came to no harm: *turn back*, at whatever personal cost to themselves that might eventually entail. No, that was asking too much, after they'd come all this way, and would make a mockery of the emotional certainty and total physical communion they'd awakened and fomented in the time they'd had together since her arrival at his house beyond the airstrip the morning before . . . So, in uneasy acceptance of their fate and to prepare her for at least some of the exigencies she must expect to encounter and have to contend with *en route* —

"Kisangani," he said. "Over the border into the Congo, the first town you reach of any size. I know for a fact there's a consulate there." And he went on, "You tell them you've had your passport stolen and they'll issue you with a temporary travel document — in any name you like to choose — to take you at least as far as Leopoldville."

"Mm, that's more or less what I had in mind," she said. "Only, in Leopoldville, I don't go anywhere near our Embassy, do I, but use my temporary pass to get on a flight to the UK, or somewhere else?"

"To the UK direct, if you can," he said. "But with a stopover or two if necessary, all right that shouldn't matter. It's just getting that initial flight out from Leopoldville which could prove very tricky without a real passport in your hand. Don't try it with BOAC, whatever you do."

"I thought," she said, "that if I'm lucky and very careful to pick the right man, I ought to be able to bribe my way through. Belgian emigration officials, a foreign national going home, a young woman —"

"Christ," he said evenly, "maybe, maybe not. And you make one mistake with that you could be in big trouble, possibly face arrest."

"Then?"

"Then?" he repeated, thinking it over for long moments but failing to come up with anything better. "All I can say is, may God be with you. I don't like it, though, my love, I have to admit."

"Neither do I, not that much. Not now when it's only an hour or two before that bus leaves."

"You're the bravest of the brave," he said, giving her a squeeze. "My thoughts will go with you every step of your journey."

"Not brave," she said quietly. "Merely stubborn. Determined somehow to make it home and wait for you there, in hope."

"You'll cable me, won't you, as soon as you get back?"

"Cable, and write, to give you my address. Maybe write, from Nairobi, or elsewhere, on my travels, to let you know how I'm getting on."

"You do that, yes, please," he said. "Please try."

"But, once I'm home, I shouldn't write too often, I suppose," she went on thoughtfully, "and I'd better type my letters, hadn't I?" And, with an attempt at a smile, "I ought to have another name, too. Why don't you choose one for me?"

After a second he said, "Francesca", because he'd always found it evocative.

"Some old flame?" she queried. "If so I'd like to scratch her eyes out, and won't use it — so confess."

"Never known any girl called Francesca," he said, "That's a promise. But it suits you, I think."

"All right, Francesca it is," she said. "I'm F, or Francesca — or even Frankie — a doting cousin, from this day on."

They were descending a long slope, in early morning daylight, the trees and jungle still on their right and, for once, a broad and precipitous ravine on their left. Ahead of them, at a corner, a huge outcrop of lichened rock towered up and masked any sight of the road beyond. The trees marched up and over it, but the ravine, or fault in the land, continued on into the distance as far as the eye could see.

He slowed a little and swung the wheel to negotiate the corner, the huge rock looming above them and, on the opposite side of it, without the slightest warning, drove straight into a herd of elephant. In the middle of the road, no more than three yards away, was a baby, very young and, though he stamped on the brakes, fought the wheel round, he couldn't stop in time or avoid it, and slammed into it side on, knocking it down. At once the herd was upon them, ringing the vehicle: a big tusker, trumpeting — as frightening a sound as any on earth — three matriarchs, half-a-dozen youngsters, all bent on revenge and retribution. While one of the matriarchs saw to the fallen baby, raised it to its feet and shooed it away, the tusker and the other matriarchs went for their stalled and defenceless vehicle, giving them no chance. Using his great tusks, trunk and forehead, the tusker, aided and abetted by the remaining females, levered the Land Rover over on its side, the two of them tumbling about and struggling to hang on, then shoved at it, rocked it, and propelled it to the edge of the ravine where, in a final surge of brute strength and violence, they tipped it over.

They rolled and plummeted forty feet down but, miraculously, didn't catch fire. At one point, halfway to the depths and their canopy torn off, she was thrown out: a ragdoll in the shape and guise of a near-naked woman flying through the air, keening. Mercifully, the plunging vehicle missed her, didn't come down on top of her as it smashed and rattled on through the stunted trees and matted undergrowth below.

He should have been killed but, with the steering-wheel to cling on to, somehow pure good fortune dictated he survived. Not even seriously injured, merely knocked about and badly bruised, he extricated himself from the wrecked vehicle when it came to a jolting stop at the bottom of the ravine. Stood shaking and holding his left elbow, in the half-light down there as, shocked and bewildered at his deliverance, he recovered his breath and got his bearings. Then he went looking for her, shouting her name; stumbling, falling, picking himself up as he forced his way past obstacles, over rock and through waist-high undergrowth, climbing all the time, in search of her. A picture in his mind, to torture him, of his last sight of her, his girl, the way she'd been reclining in the Land Rover's cab beside him, their forward planning, as far as it could be, rehearsed, and anxieties, at least for the time being, put on hold, only moments before the elephant struck. Her bare feet had been up on the fascia, her shirt unbuttoned, her knees wide and skirt rolled up over her naked thighs, because she'd been hot and sweaty after their recent loving and even hotter between her legs. Oh Jesus, Jeanne — oh God, I beg you — I *beg* you, *please*.

He found her splayed out in the shadows, her wailing and terrified ejection and descent halted by a barrier of half-grown saplings; the rock-hard terrain in which these were rooted had produced growth that was resilient enough to break her fall — likewise her body, and in all probability her back. She was lying at an unnatural angle, partly on her side, but she wasn't dead. Her shirt had been torn from her, she was naked to the waist, bleeding from her mouth and ears and one eye-socket was a dark pool of blood. She also had a deep and bleeding gash beneath her ribs. Nevertheless, she was trying to move, moaning, making scrabbling and futile gestures with the clawing fingers of her left hand before, gradually, they ceased altogether and she went limp.

Clumsily he knelt beside her; bent down and, without thinking, tried to insinuate his good arm beneath her to roll her gently on to her back and get a better look at her. But, at his intrusive touch, she groaned once in agony and, cursing himself, he immediately desisted, withdrew his hands and sat back, attempting — in horror — to take stock of her condition, and realizing soon enough that if she weren't to die, there was no way of helping her where she lay. Praying the elephant herd would be gone, he had to get her back up to the road, if he could. So, pleading, "I'm sorry, I'm sorry, I have to do it," he got his good arm under her again, this time successfully; then, with a grunting exhalation of breath and the limited help of his other hand which was painful and not working too well, he lifted her inert and seemingly lifeless body, contriving to turn it over as he did so, until she hung, head lolling, legs and feet dangling down, but the weight of her broken body supported in his arms.

He clutched her to him as best he could, lifting her head and pressing her face gently against his chest. Began to climb, one jerky step, then the next, up the steep bank. She wasn't really heavy, no, a slim beautifully built girl, but the state he was in, weakened by shock and exhaustion, almost too heavy for him. He had to stop often, grit his teeth and recover his will, gather renewed strength, to keep on going, start climbing again. Nearly, several times, stumbling, he dropped her, but knew, even as waves of faintness and despair clouded and darkened his vision, that he must not put her down, worse still let her fall, because to pick her up and try again was now almost certainly beyond him. Once or twice he checked her breathing, halting and lowering his head; found each time that although still unconscious she was indeed breathing, shallowly and fast. He gave thanks for that and it spurred him to further effort, staggering on, foothold by precarious foothold: choosing what appeared to him the best route to avoid loose scree, heavy undergrowth and other hazards in his path. Slowly and painfully he fought his way up, his own pain *nothing* compared with what hers must have been like but a short while before. Up again. Until, the light improving with every foot he gained but still taken by surprise, he found they'd nearly made it, were almost up to the level of the main road. In one final effort, his feet dragging and arms numb by this time, he mounted the last few ledges of crumbling rock and came to a halt, swaying and struggling for breath, on the stony poorly grassed verge which, thereabouts, was little more than a yard wide.

There were scuffmarks, skidmarks, huge footprints across the part-gravelled murram roadway to his right, back in the direction of that huge outcrop of rock round which they'd come to meet disaster head on, and the sun risen behind it now, casting its dark and menacing shadow along the road to his feet. But no elephant, not one in sight — thank God! — so apparently the herd had indeed taken off, having done its worst. Dreadfully afraid and his back and shoulders aching unmercifully, he looked down and examined what was left of her once beautiful, still slender and moving but now grossly injured and contorted body lying senseless in his arms. Confirmed with one sickening glance his worst fears, the appalling nature of the wounds to her face and head: the left eye gone in a welter of blood and tissue, the cheek beneath it blackened and grotesquely swollen, her cheekbone smashed and her mouth twisted out of shape with broken teeth showing through blood still leaking between torn lips, runnelling down her jaw, beneath her ear and into her hair. Her once-entrancing and beloved face was transformed, disfigured beyond recognition or hope of restoration, God help her. There was a light breeze but the sour-sweet smell of her caught at his throat: the pungent cloying reek of blood and urine soaking her ruckled skirt. It was this second and more revealing *sight* of her, in the clear light of a new day, which almost unmanned him, made him shudder and sob out loud, as sadness overwhelmed him; also warned him she had to be close to death. But she was still breathing — he lowered his head again to make sure — so there yet remained some faint residue of hope she might live, if only he could get her to a doctor, a surgeon, before it was too late.

He had three choices: to lay her down on soft ground, if he could find any, cover her and keep her warm, until the arrival maybe after several hours of a passing vehicle, truck or Land Rover, in which to transport her to some clinic or hospital. But, in these parts, no vehicle might turn up for many hours. Or to carry her along the road, towards Mingida — maybe fifteen miles away — until he came to a village where the people could make her a stretcher, and he could hire and persuade men to carry her on. Or to carry her as far as that sizeable village — five miles or so back — where there had been a Posts and Telegraphs office, and from there wire Langoro and tell David Morgan where he was, that he'd broken down, and ask the DC please to send Joseph out. But, although tempted by this third option, it wasn't a good one, he concluded, for many and diverse reasons, the principal one being that at Langoro Dr Silvarosa wasn't any kind of surgeon, and it was surgery she needed, transfusions, trained nursing, none of which Langoro could provide, and needed quickly if she were to have any chance of survival. So not that way, no, and he could not wait for the possibility of a passing vehicle, either, but would walk it, carrying her in his arms, without water and while his strength lasted — he'd *make* it last! — in the hope that the next village on the way to Mingida wasn't far, and take it from there. Get to Mingida as soon as he could where, being a much bigger place than Langoro, he remembered, there was more than one doctor, one of whom might well be a qualified surgeon, though he didn't know that for a fact, and the hospital and nursing facilities were both in a different class from those on the little outstation where he had lived and worked and where he had first found and loved her with a physical certainty, passion and sundering of past ties which had seemed destined and set fair to change his life. Well, it would do that now, but not in the way intended, that was for sure. No, very cruelly, what they were into now was a different scenario altogether.

So be it and God help him through whatever lay ahead; that was what he was going to do, *try* to do: get them to Mingida as there was no tolerable alternative. He'd do it, therefore, somehow, and start at once. But he was experienced enough, and had his wits sufficiently about him again, to realize he had to have water, a canteen of it at least, for his own use and hers, if he could trickle a little down her throat, in case he had to carry her for miles in the sun; in case they crossed no stream on the way. There'd been canteens in the car prior to its descent into hell, also a blanket, digger hats, and maybe, just possibly, he could find them again.

How They Fared

J. F. BENNING OBE

13.6.56 Suspended from duties

14.7.56 Following investigation by senior officers from Lindi and Dar-es-Salaam, formally and severely reprimanded, replaced at Langoro and transferred to the capital, pending instructions from London.

28.8.56 In light of ensuing and adverse publicity, he resigned the service and was immediately sent home.

01.1957–06.1978 Patrol Officer/ADO/District Officer, Dept. of Native Affairs, Papua New Guinea (Sepik Dist., Konedobu, Mt Hagen, Lae). Honoured in recognition of selfless leadership, involving hands-on rescue and resettlement work following giant volcanic eruption on Manam Island, off northern coast, 1974. Retired, aged 48, and returned to the UK, in search of a different career closer to home.

— m. Barbara Johnston, Australian national,

1962; two children, a boy and a girl. Divorced 1969; mother granted custody of the children and later remarried.

1979–80 One year Postgraduate Course (TEFL), self-financed, at London Institute of Education.

1980–89 Contract English Language Teacher/ Inspector, sponsored by the British Council, Beirut, Oman, Qatar, Saudi Arabia.
— m. Christine Yazigy, Lebanese Christian national (aged 25) 1982. No children. She deserted him in 1984 and joined relatives already established in San Diego, California, USA.

1991–2006 Collaborator/co-author EFL textbooks, audiovisual material, etc, for series *Highways* (McGinley, Chaudury, Benning) first published 1997.

J. D. MORGAN

1955–57 District Commissioner, Langoro. Handled aftermath of Benning affair locally, meticulously following instructions from his superiors.

1957–65 Transferred to Tukuyu (Southern Highlands Province) as DC and, in due course, at Iringa and Mbeya.
— wife, Patti, left him in 1958, from whom unable to obtain a divorce. Died 1963 — murdered — a celebrated case —

	on safari with current lover, a tobacco farmer, outside Bulawayo, Southern Rhodesia.
1965	(following Independence) Opted for early retirement, golden handshake, pension, and returned home to South Africa.
1965–86	Labour Relations Officer, later consultant, with Manson Van Staay Mining Corporation, based at Bloemfontein and Jo'burg. — m. Charlotte Reinach, South African national, 1968. She died 1981 after a long illness.
1986–2006	Retired to smallholding near Port Elizabeth, Cape Province, where he cultivated tomatoes commercially and became involved in local politics.

GWEN PARMINTER (MOTHER LIVIA)

09.1956	Removed from her position at Mtina by mission authorities and mission station closed down, following investigation into irregularities there. Accepted subordinate position at mission station in Rajasthan, India. Died 1961 of enteric fever.

FATHER SIMON (former lieutenant-colonel, RA)

10.1956	Offered early retirement and returned to the UK and civilian life.
02.1959	Committed suicide. Laid to rest in country churchyard in W. Midlands. Quiet

ceremony, paid for by his old regiment, attended by half-a-dozen ex-officers and other ranks.

NUSSOULA ALI MANDINGO

1959 Appointed Head Messenger, Langoro,

12.1964 Left government service after Independence and returned to his home village on the Rovuma. As a young man he had offered his allegiance to the British whom he looked up to and was prepared to work with and serve to the best of his ability, to the extent of alerting them, if the need arose, to the deceptions and sometimes primitive practices indulged in by his own people. A brave man — almost uneducated — who, on occasion, was ready to face down the ignorance and tribalism which tended to get in the way of what he believed to be progress and good governance, during his time at District HQ he played a significant supporting role in the advancement of Langoro and earned the trust and liking of more than one committed administrator. However, with Independence, came *foreign* Africans to take over the running of his district. He neither welcomed them nor was he willing to fall in with their often unprincipled agendas and he decided he wanted no further part in ongoing developments which meant all too frequently, stagnation or a return to the past.

A strong personality, short-tempered and not easy to get along with, at his village he disdained to take part in local affairs, cultivated his land, smuggled ivory, and thereby acquired considerable wealth.

1980 Died of blackwater fever, a morose and embittered man.

SALIM MOHAMED GWAYA

1956–61 Served two DOs after John Benning as cook/houseboy both faithfully and well; the odd perks here, the odd perks there, never mind; he never overdid it, and had been generously rewarded by Benning prior to his departure. Married second, and much younger, wife during this time, by whom he fathered two children.

1963 During year of drought and crop failure, he received small pension from the government but eventually was forced to sell his house and land outside Langoro town for a pittance and went to live with his half-brother at Namwea. Having little in common the two men didn't get on.

1972 Died of snakebite, treatment for which, apart from traditional *dawa*, not available at that time.

KAISI ISA KAMBONA

10.1956	An adventurous boy, and without a word to his family, he took what was left of Benning's gratuity to him and headed for Lindi. There he lived on his wits for a couple of months before being taken on, for little more than his keep, on an Omani trading dhow on its way to the Comorros.
1957–74	Based latterly in Zanzibar made his life at sea and became a skilled and experienced navigator, visiting ports as far north as Busheir and as far south as Beira.
09.1974	Disappeared, and his body never found, when the dhow he was skippering — and of which he was part-owner — was lost with all hands in a freak storm off Socotra.

JOSEPH BENEDICTUS ULAYA

1956–60	Continued as highly competent, resourceful and uncommonly gifted government mechanic at Langoro. In due course recovered Benning's wrecked vehicle from the ravine at roadside on the way to Mingida and, having obtained the ex-DO's ungrudging permission to do so before his transfer, held on to it for spares, some of which he sold on, and then let it go for scrap. His occasional, racially satisfying and lucrative liaison with Patti Morgan,

	the DC's wife, ended in 1957 when her husband was posted to Tukuyu.
1960	Left government service to work for Jaydeeco Bus Co. at Lindi as head mechanic at much increased salary.
1964	Returned north to his home village on Tanganyika/Kenya border. Started small-scale profitable vehicle repair and trucking business beside nearby international main road.
1973–77	Sold out and retired to his village where, four years later, his sexual powers and personal magnetism both waning and with little to do, he died of boredom and prostate cancer.

LA'ALI SELEMANI MAHENGE

10.1956	When Mtina closed, returned to village with small gratuity.
1957	Gave birth to child, a girl, by Joseph Ulaya who, afterwards, sent her a little money from time to time in support. Treated with reserve bordering on contempt by local villagers and unable to find a husband.
1960	Went to Masasi with her child and begged the help of the same missionary society she had worked for before. Found position as nanny to three young children of Greek road foreman by previous dissolved

marriage. Became his mistress. He beat her.

1966 When her lover/protector was facing arrest on charges of corruption and fled the country she was left destitute and returned to her home village where when opportunity offered she sold her body to keep herself and her growing child. Also earned a little money as a seamstress.

1968 Believed killed by leopard near village bathing place. Her remains never found.

ELIZABETH PAULINE CANNING

09.1956 Broke off engagement to John Benning over the phone in London, at his insistence, not hers.

01.1957 Married, happily, second son of wine importing family whom she had been seeing for some time. Shortly afterwards moved to the Charente, France, where she and her husband, a French citizen, settled and thereafter only rarely returned to the UK.

JEANNE MICHAELA RAWSON (SISTER CARMELA)

10.06.1956 Died of wounds/internal injuries at Lindi General Hospital. Buried — no ceremony — at the old German cemetery outside town, John Benning unable to be present.

Interment costs and later simple headstone paid for by Benning on his way through to the capital on transfer.

1965 Her grave vandalized and bones scattered, along with those of many others and, apart from a few tumbling walls, cemetery reverted to bush.

To the WahiYao — Mattaka, Kandulu, Kundenda — of Southern Province, Tanzania, in memory of a time that was.

Particularly: Albert Mwanjesa
Ismail Ausi MC
Wait Njaidi MC
Saidi Mwichande
Marion Matola
(RIP)

Author's Note

Fearful of what might lie in prospect, just prior to Independence, the Kandulu Yao took off en masse for Portuguese East Africa where they hoped they'd be left in peace.

Also available in ISIS Large Print:

Under a Sapphire Sky

Susannah Bates

Talented Marianne and gregarious Gabby have been friends since college. It feels natural to go into business together, selling Marianne's unique jewellery designs, and their family ties become closer when Marianne falls in love with charismatic stone-dealer Jay, Gabby's half-brother. But as their company takes off, Gabby's contribution becomes more questionable. Meanwhile, Marianne is blossoming and she is expecting Jay's baby.

Then Marianne's ex-boyfriend Paul walks back into her life in search of an engagement ring for his new fiancée. Marianne discovers to her cost that, like the beautiful stones she works with, relationships too can hold fatal hidden flaws. In the tropical heat of southern Sri Lanka, she begins to see that the finest quality often lies buried in unlikely places, and to realise that someone she once easily dismissed might be the only person who can save her . . .

ISBN 978-0-7531-8634-3 (hb)
ISBN 978-0-7531-8635-0 (pb)

Mrs Tim of the Regiment

D. E. Stevenson

Vivacious, young Hester Christie tries to run her home like clockwork, as would befit the wife of British Army officer, Tim Christie. However hard Mrs Tim strives for seamless living, she is always moving flat out to remember groceries, rule lively children, side-step village gossip and placate her husband with bacon, eggs, toast and marmalade. Left alone for months at a time whilst her husband is with his regiment, Mrs Tim resolves to keep a diary of family life.

When a move to a new regiment in Scotland uproots the Christie family, Mrs Tim is hurled into a whole new drama of dilemmas. Against the wild landscape of surging rivers, sheer rocks and rolling mists, who should stride into Mrs Tim's life one day but the dashing Major Morley. Hester will soon find that life holds unexpected crossroads . . .

ISBN 978-0-7531-8608-4 (hb)
ISBN 978-0-7531-8609-1 (pb)

The Secrets We Keep

Colette Caddle

It's four years since Erin Joyce left Dublin and bought a guesthouse in the remote, beautiful village of Dunbarra. The Gatehouse attracts a strange clutch of guests who, once ensconced, never want to leave. There's Hazel, a shy artist, and her sweet, silent daughter Gracie. Sandra, a brash American, wants to know everything about everyone. Then there's wise old easy-going PJ, who's seemingly part of the furniture.

But Erin's fragile happiness is thrown off-balance by the arrival of A-list Hollywood actor Sebastian Gray. Erin finds herself drawn to this handsome enigmatic man, who used to walk with a swagger but now prowls the country lanes with haunted eyes.

Sebastian isn't the only one in the Gatehouse with a secret. As Erin finds herself embroiled in her guests' secrets she starts to ask herself: will she be ready to reveal her own?

ISBN 978-0-7531-8566-7 (hb)
ISBN 978-0-7531-8567-4 (pb)

Beachcombing

Maggie Dana

Jillian Hunter treasures her independence. She's raised two sons by herself, launched a small business and restored a tumbledown beach cottage in Connecticut. But when a trip to London reunites her with Colin — an old flame she hasn't seen in 35 years — Jill falls for him all over again.

Love makes Jill reckless. This could be her chance for a new beginning. But Colin isn't quite the boy she remembers and she ends up risking everything she's worked for — her business, her home and her two closest friends — to make a life with him. And when she's faced with the risk of losing Colin as well, Jill is forced to take an uncomfortably close look at the woman she's allowed herself to become.

ISBN 978-0-7531-8622-0 (hb)
ISBN 978-0-7531-8623-7 (pb)

A Time for Every Season

Shelagh Noden

Meg Fraser, widowed in the early weeks of World War I, has vowed to preserve the family farm for her son, Will, and daughter, Isobel, but has made a dangerous enemy in neighbour Dod Grant, who has designs on the farm, and her. He makes it plain that he can ruin the business if she continues to oppose him.

Later, when Dod is found dead, Will is accused of murder, and Isobel, distraught at the news that David, her fiancé, is missing in action, falls dangerously ill. Meg has to turn for help to the one man she thought she could never face again. It will take all her reserves of courage and resilience to bring the family through these difficult times.

ISBN 978-0-7531-8546-9 (hb)
ISBN 978-0-7531-8547-6 (pb)